Another *Twist* of Lyme

~

David Ruffle

Paperback ISBN 9781780926506
ePub ISBN 9781780926513
PDF ISBN 9781780926520

Published in the UK by MX Publishing
335 Princess Park Manor, Royal Drive, London, N11 3GX
www.mxpublishing.com

Cover layout and construction by
www.staunch.com

Also by David Ruffle

Sherlock Holmes and the Lyme Regis Horror

Sherlock Holmes and the Lyme Regis Horror (expanded 2nd Edition)

Sherlock Holmes and the Lyme Regis Legacy

Holmes and Watson: End Peace

Sherlock Holmes and the Lyme Regis Trials

The Abyss (A Journey with Jack the Ripper)

A Twist of Lyme

Sherlock Holmes: The Lyme Regis Trilogy (Illustrated Omnibus Edition)

For Children

Sherlock Holmes and the Missing Snowman (illustrated by Rikey Austin)

As editor and contributor

Tales from the Stranger's Room (Vol.1)

Tales from the Stranger's Room (Vol. 2)

3

For Melody

Family faces are magic mirrors. Looking at people who belong to us, we see the past, present, and future.
~*Gail Lumet Buckley*

In time of test, family is best.
~*Burmese Proverb*

Meet the Hamiltons. (Again)

Michael Hamilton 46 Reviewer. Husband of below.

Judy Hamilton 44 Writer. Wife of above. Mother of below.

Katy Hamilton 13 School pupil. Daughter of above. Sister of below.

Annabelle Hamilton 11 School pupil. Sister of above.

Formerly living: Greater London.

Now living: Lyme Regis.

Read on to learn even more…as we move between present day and the recent past.

Book One

Chapter One-Present Day

Michael Hamilton was in a reflective mood. This would be surprising to many people who knew him well, to many people who knew him only moderately well and perhaps even to himself. He was not generally given to reflective moods or deep thinking. Not an easy thing to admit at forty-six years of age yet there it was; an incontrovertible fact. Here he was, however, reflecting.

"You're looking in a reflective mood, Mike," said Judy, his wife of sixteen years who had learned a thing or two about Michael in the course of their married and pre-married lives.

"Maybe it's because I am, Jude."

"You?" she queried, but only a little scornfully. Scorn had never played a big part in their relationship and she saw no need to introduce it at this stage. Not fully anyway.

"Yes, me! Is that so strange?"

"Well, a little," Judy replied, but marginally less scornfully. "You know who you remind me of, don't you?"

"Henry Kissinger?"

"No, silly, one of those characters in novels who are busy reflecting on their lives in order to make those who didn't buy the first book less guilty about knowing nothing about them. By succinctly summing up the whole of their existence in a paragraph or two, they introduce the characters and sub-history to the reader yet not in enough detail to stop said reader from dashing out to buy the first novel in the series. For instance," she said, barely pausing to take breath or account of her husband's puzzled expression. "You, Mike, would be reflecting on how we met on that fateful day at Clapham Junction station, your somewhat awkward proposal, your job at '*The Big Brash Guide to London*', my dalliances with Christopher Drummond and Jason Wilkins, your encounter with Mrs (?) Sheila Barry, Katy and Annie coming along and how we moved to Lyme and encountered our resident ghosts. As well as your childhood, hayricks and imaginary heroes. You see, I have it all worked out."[1]

"Sounds like a character in a second-rate novel to me."

"And to me."

"Well, you should know after all."

It was a remark he instantly regretted, but not instantly enough. He had lately discovered a disconcerting propensity to say hugely inappropriate things, not to mention inaccurate. Even more disconcerting was a propensity to hurt the ones he loved. Judy bore the brunt of this. As she did on this occasion. He stumbled on, thinking an apology may only serve to exaggerate the insult. And taking it back an even more tacit confession it had been made at all. Michael didn't always find life easy.

---

[1] See 'A Twist of Lyme' to learn more. Please!

"All of which may be true if I were a fictional character and actually thinking about those events. But as I am not and was not, your notion is shot down in flames."

"Then what were you thinking about?"

"My father."

"Ah."

Judy's 'ah' was not a puzzled ah; it was an all-knowing ah. Her response may have been heavy on brevity, but it was fuelled with the knowledge and understanding of her man and as such that single ah could have filled a book. But not this one.

Michael's father, Geoffrey Hamilton had passed away several months ago. A combination of a broken heart, Alzheimer's and lung disease carried him off although he had been ailing steadily over the previous six years since his wife, Michael's mother, Margaret died. The house and stables had been sold and a former stable-hand had offered to take Geoffrey into her house in Chipping Norton[2]. He did not want for care in his final years. In truth, he needed very little for his mind was in a permanent fog with only occasional flashes of light in which the old Geoffrey shone through, well, as much as he ever shone anyway.

In the spirit, if not the word of apology, Michael asked, "How is the new novel coming along, Jude?"

---

[2] A bustling, buzzing market town in the Cotswolds. It boasts the oldest golf course in Oxfordshire. So there

10

"Not too badly thanks. It's a relief to get back into writing…after…well…you know. I almost lost the will to ever pick up a pen again. Well, use the keyboard that is, but you know what I mean."[3]

Michael knew what she meant. He was good like that. Michael never did write the novel he promised himself and everybody else he would. Judy in fact, had taken up the writing reins three years previously and had two books out there in the wide world doing their thing. The second one had nudged into the best-seller lists which surprised Judy, her publisher and Michael, possibly in that order. Possibly not.

The first two books, *Game On* and *Game, Set and Match* were set in the world of professional tennis with the added glamour of espionage and various bouts of skulduggery. Judy saw no reason to change this winning if puzzling combination. She had seen however, a good enough reason to stop work and become a full-time writer, but she was ever conscious of the fact it had been Michael's dream and not her own. To Michael's chagrin, Judy had not consulted him about the world of espionage in spite of his familiarity with Johnny Stevens, secret agent extraordinaire. Admittedly, Johnny Stevens was entirely fictitious and furthermore had resided in Michael's head for nigh on thirty-five years. Even so, he felt he could have been of some use. Michael didn't always find being on the side-lines easy. In a neat reversal of the roles they had become accustomed to, she became the house-wife, house-mother and Michael returned to the wonders of the world of employment. He once more became the man to come to for reviews.

---

[3] All will be revealed in Book Two.

11

Any other changes you wonder? Of course.

Katy is now fast (very) approaching her thirteenth birthday and the changes that will bring. She has battles with dyslexia and inherited dodgy knees that she bears stoically without blaming her parents once, whether that would remain the case into her teenage years, time will tell. The sibling rivalry between Katy and Annabelle was at times a gulf in itself, but Katy becoming a teenager threatens to turn it into a veritable chasm. The roles of elder sister-younger sister are about to be redefined by what Katy likes to think is her new found maturity. This gap between them would widen for a few years to come, but as their twenties beckoned, they would find that no one knew or indeed cared who was the elder or younger. Most of all, themselves.

"I can hardly believe that Katy is going to be thirteen. Where has all that time gone?"

"Tell me about it," answered Mike although Judy had just done precisely that. "But my guess is that it won't change her."

"Mike, my poor deluded hero. It would not surprise me at all if she were to come up with a list of special privileges that she feels she will be entitled to along with her new status."

"You think?"

"No, of course not. I was teasing you, my teasable hero."

Being a father was wonderful, but at times unfathomable for Michael. Just when he thought he knew his daughters, something would happen to cause him to question it. They were of course ever-changing and Michael had to change and adapt with them. He knew that, but still found it difficult to adjust. He didn't always find adjusting easy. Perhaps he never would.

"Where is Katy this evening anyway?"

"At a birthday party. I did tell you, Mike. I am picking her up at eight."

"And Annie?"

"Homework hopefully. Are you not with it at all this evening?"

"Apparently not," he answered and instantly wished he hadn't. But not instantly enough.

"Your dad?"

"Yes, Jude. I'll tell you about it later. It's gone seven-thirty; do you want me to collect Katy?"

"I'll do it, it's fine."

The birthday party was being held in a rather grand house just off the Sidmouth Road. Judy arrived at the same time as all the other parents (all mothers oddly enough). The sound of music (not the film) could be heard blaring out. Hardly music at all, thought Judy who still occasionally pined for the boy bands of her youth. Even Bros[4]. Very odd. Eventually, she had no choice, but to vacate the warmth of her car and wander from room to room in search of Katy. The house seemed cavernous, but less so than it could have done

---

[4] A band of the late 80's and early 90's built around the twin brothers Luke and Matt Goss.

being full of teenagers (thirty-four girls, six boys). Katy suddenly appeared. Judy smelt her breath.

"God, mum, stop it. I haven't been drinking!"

Judy could not think of an alternative reason to put forward to Katy as to why she had felt the need to smell her breath so she did not try. The journey home became a conversation free zone, but Katy burst into life as soon as they entered the house.

"I've got something for you," she announced, thrusting a sheet of paper into her dad's hand.

"Ah," exclaimed Michael. "Look here, Jude, it's a list of special privileges our daughter feel she is entitled to. Well, well."

Judy scanned the sheet and mentally devised her answers. Michael had already decided to say no to everything without reading any of it, but decided at the last moment to read it through.

"Let's see now shall we," said Michael, now scanning the sheet also after being nudged by Judy.

"No. No. No. You want what, young lady? No. Maybe. No chance. What time? No. You have to be joking. No. Maybe. Yes (how surprising is that?). No. Ha-ha. No."

"Mum?" appealed Katy.

"Sorry, I'm with your dad on this. Where did you get all this from?"

"The TeenRights website. See, I know my rights!"

14

"Teen rights indeed," sighed Michael. "Have you got homework to do? If so I suggest you go and do it and stop being so silly."

"Life's so unfair," shouted Katy as she flounced upstairs in the way that teenagers do. She had been practising and in two days' time she will be found to have perfected it. The cry of pain on the stairs came from Annabelle whose only sin was to be coming down as Katy was going up. Katy had already perfected the art of kicking her sister in the shin. It was the result of all the painstaking hours of practice.

"We have created a monster!"

"Yes, Mike, I have a feeling the next few years are going to be fun all the way! But then…life is always fun with you. Just a little different too at times."

Chapter Two-A Funeral

St Andrew's Church[5]. Great Rollright. The final resting place of Geoffrey Hamilton and his wife, Margaret. It would have been the resting place of his current favourite horse too, but the local veterinary surgeon, the ecclesiastical authorities, Michael and Judy had all combined to consign that particular codicil to history.

For someone who had lived a long life, the congregation was disconcertingly small. But then, Geoffrey at eighty-six had outlived many of his friends and seen off all his family with the exception of Michael, Judy, Katy and Annabelle. The cheese and wine party brigade who had been in evidence at the magisterial Margaret's funeral were conspicuous by their absence at Geoffrey's. Although the turn-out was poor the send-off was good. The vicar, Howard Felling did a splendid job in spite of his lack of knowledge of Geoffrey. Michael had given him a few pointers which now fell out of his mouth into the (small) congregation. Not literally. That would be hideous.

"Geoffrey may have been curmudgeonly at times, but his heart was in the right place."

---

[5] A fabulous church with an equally fabulous carved Norman doorway.

'Curmudgeonly? Well, I suppose he could.' Next to him, Judy was nodding vigorously so there seemed to be no doubt on that score...he was often curmudgeonly.

"Geoffrey truly loved Margaret and his horses."

'Hold on there. Someone missing surely.' Michael looked up in an attempt to get the vicar's eye. He gave him a look which had 'what about me?' imprinted all over it. Michael didn't always find giving meaningful looks easy. Nor apparently did Howard Felling whose own meaningful look was lost on Michael. As we said...

"Geoffrey, of course, also loved his son, Michael."

'Also? Also? He makes me sound like some kind of appendage,' thought Michael. He shot the vicar another look which he hoped would convey all this. The vicar shot Michael another look which once again meant nothing to Michael. Judy shot a look at Michael. He understood Judy's look only too well. It was *the* look. He immersed himself in his thoughts as the vicar spoke at some length. He was so deeply immersed in them that he missed his cue from the vicar, inviting him to say a few words. Another look, *the* look from Judy roused him.

At first, the words would not come. Come on, pull yourself together. Would Johnny Norfolk be struck dumb when asked to say a few words about the late Chief Executive of the FA? Would Johnny Stevens be reduced to a wreck because he had to praise the recently deceased head of MI6? He cleared his throat.

"To tell the truth, I haven't really planned what to say other than Dad was a simple, decent man who was devoted to my mother and worked hard to help provide for her and for me. There were no frills with Dad, what you saw was what you got. Anyone who ever

17

saw his battered Land-Rover Defender can testify to that. I have no anecdotes to tell, his life did not encourage witty tales and vignettes, but he enjoyed his life and was always giving of his time and energy. And why do I feel as though I have not said as much as I can about a man who lived eighty-six years? I don't feel that I have done justice to the man, but conversely I feel I have said all I want to say. Thank you all of you and thank you, dad."

He returned to his seat, both relieved and a little bit proud of himself. Judy kissed him; even in church it was by far the most appropriate response. Tom Kennedy squeezed his shoulder, quite some effort on his part as he was sitting two pews behind Michael. Katy squeezed his hand, showing herself not yet to be the monster that Michael and Judy will later think they had created. Annabelle smiled.

The vicar led the way out into the churchyard to a small plot in the south-east corner where Geoffrey would be laid to rest. The grey clouds had parted allowing a little weak sunshine to filter through on this, the last act in the life of Geoffrey Hamilton. The small congregation and a neighbouring sheep looked on, the congregation respectfully and the sheep inquisitively. The vicar invited all present (not including the sheep) to offer up a silent prayer to a God Michael was sure that none of those present believed in with the probable, but by no means certain, exception of Howard Felling.

Barbara Hale who had served in the role as Geoffrey's carer for the last few months had provided some refreshments at her house in West Street, Chipping Norton.

"Don't you be expecting too much from me will you?" she said, to each guest as they entered her humble yet homely house.

She was assured nobody was.

Barbara, who, unlike Michael, had always enjoyed doing something with horses, whatever that something was and had begun work at the stables many, many years ago. After retiring she had kept in touch with Geoffrey and Margaret throughout the intervening years. It was she who suggested to Michael that she take his father in, a good friend is never a burden she assured him and it would award Geoffrey a kind of continuity in his final months. A familiar face and familiar Cotswolds surroundings, even if it was destined to become increasingly unfamiliar to him in his final months.

The refreshments that Barbara had provided hit the spot. Everyone said so. Barbara beamed at one and all; she had never seen so many people in her house apart from that never to be forgotten day when her garden was rumoured to be the scene of an attempted alien abduction just a few days after a UFO had been spotted hovering over the town. Needless to say there was no truth in any of it, aliens have never been particularly enamoured of visiting the Cotswolds, but even so the Chipping Norton town council voted not to compensate her for her trampled petunias.

"Would you like to come upstairs, Michael?" she asked.

Momentarily, Michael had flashbacks to Pimlico and Mrs (?) Sheila Barry, who offered up a similar invitation, but with connotations that Barbara Hale would not even be distantly aware of.

"I have some things of your father's you may like," she added.

Geoffrey had moved into her house with very few possessions save for clothes (most of which he never needed) and books (most of which he never read). The house and stables in Adlestrop[6] had been sold along with the fixtures and fittings, all with Geoffrey's blessing. Barbara handed Michael a pile of exercise books with a rubber band tied around them. Seven in all.

"Do you know what these are, Michael?"

He resisted the temptation to say exercise books; this woman had done nothing to merit such sarcasm. "What are they?"

"Your father's poetry."

"His what?"

He opened books at random. Page after page were filled with poems, scraps of poems, short stories and musings on life which presented a whole new side to his father that he never knew existed.

"I'll leave you to it," said Barbara, softy closing the door as she left the room.

Michael was only dimly aware of her leaving the room; he was lost in this new found world of discovery. He read on…

The day draws to a close,
The night feels its way, slowly seductively forward.
Light slips away silently tiptoeing behind the clouds.
Darkness holds dominion over all.
Clarity is left behind as the black night envelops the scene.
Trees sway, gentle breezes dance chattering and laughing,
But soon quietness stills the night and settles all around.
Silent, yet, still can be heard for those who care to listen,

---

[6] Adlestrop was immortalised by Edward Thomas's poem "Adlestrop" which was first published in 1917.

Voices whispering in the dark, the souls of the night.
The lights of our towns and cities blur nature's true vision,
Until once again the sun comes to reveal all,
Rising once more and the world is refreshed for the new dawn.
The day exhales and light and life is reborn.

He tried to imagine his father composing these verses as he drove around the Cotswolds in his battered Land-Rover Defender. Or as he took an early morning gallop. Or shovelling horse dung. Try as he might he could not reconcile this outpouring of emotion from the father he knew who he could not recall showing any emotion whatsoever. He read on…

Sitting in my corner
Quietly observing
The silence makes way
For the rustling passer-by
Where are you going?
Where did you come from?
Never to be seen by me again
Save for this one moment
When our paths cross
I will not remember you
You will not remember me
Our short encounter
Lost to the hands of time
Each headed in a direction our own
I am destined
Never to know your name
Nor you mine
Yet for one moment
One little second
Of all the seconds previously lived
And waiting to be lived
Our lives crossed

And we are never to be the same.

Michael wept. He wept for the father he knew. He wept for the father he had never known. He wept for the father he would never know now. When he returned downstairs it was to find everyone drifting away one by one. Judy shot him a look which was meant to convey, 'where have you been?' He found that giving her a look which would explain his absence beyond him so he took the far simpler course of just telling her.

"Come on, my brave hero, let's head home. Dad, Mum are you ready?"

They were almost ready. Tom and Elspeth were in the lounge in heated conversation with a neighbour of Barbara's, debating the charms of Chipping Norton with those of Sidmouth to where they had just retired. The arguments had raged back and forth like a high-speed tennis rally. Judy would know. It was a close run thing, but Sidmouth came out on top…just. Tom and Elspeth Kennedy left with their heads held high and Sidmouth's reputation intact.

"Thank you, Barbara, from all of us. You have been terrific through all of this. I really don't know what we would have done without you," said Michael.

"You mustn't think anything of it. It's what friends are for after all. You drive carefully. Goodbye all."

"Cheerfully," Judy said.

"I'm sorry?"

"We say drive cheerfully, not carefully."

"Why," asked Barbara.

"Er…I don't know. Does anyone know?"

No one knew.

"Well, drive cheerfully then."

"Goodbye, Barbara," was the unified and entirely accurate response from all of them.

Barbara Hale closed the front door and shut out the world once more. Alone.

Tom had driven everyone up in his people carrier with Michael taking a back seat in every sense. Should any form of navigation be required then Judy was the man for the job as it were. It was all perfectly understandable; Michael didn't always find navigating easy.

One of Katy's proposed 'special privileges' was to be allowed to stay up until eleven o' clock (she had decided she had no chance with midnight) but by nine o'clock she was sound asleep in the car leaving only Annabelle to complain about the length of the trip and Gramps's driving which she thought could be smoother with far fewer gear changes. However, being diplomatic, some of that she kept to herself before she too dropped off. By the time the lights of Lyme twinkled below them only Tom was awake which was fortunate indeed.

Chapter Three-Present Day

"What's the point in having an alarm clock if we have to call you every morning, Katy?"

"What's your problem, Dad?"

"I was under the impression I had just outlined that."

"I'm up...I am never late for school, chill out."

"You are only up because we called you....you are never late for school because, guess what? We call you."

Annabelle was sitting at the table shooting looks at her dad which were meant to convey 'don't bring me into this'. Michael of course didn't always find deciphering looks easy and stumbled blindly on and duly brought Annabelle into it.

"Look at your sister..."

Katy duly looked at her sister, she was good like that, albeit venomously in this instance.

"We don't have to call Annie a dozen times. She always gets up in plenty of time."

An audible groan from Annabelle filled the *spacious and still modernised* kitchen. A swift kick in the shin from Katy resulted in a yet more audible moan.

"Girls!" groaned an exasperated Michael. He seemed to say it so often. Indeed, he did say it often. "Stop that and get yourselves off to school, I have work to do."

"What is it today, dad?" asked Annabelle (you knew it would be Annabelle).

"I'm attending the opening of a museum near Exeter. It's dedicated to the pig farmers of lowland Devon with waxwork pigs and hands-on exhibitions on how to fatten pigs yet leave them happy and content. Or something like that. This afternoon your Nan has invited me to Sidmouth to see the latest exhibition of flower-arranging, this time built around a cricket theme by the WI members there. Or something like that. I suspect your Gramps's involvement. Are you both still here?"

They were. Nibbling toast. Sipping tea. Giving each other looks that they knew so well even if their dad did not.

"Are you still here?" asked Judy as she entered the room.

They vanished in an instant.

"Hey Jude, how do you do that?"

"Naturally gifted I guess."

"I'm attending the opening of a museum near Exeter. It's dedicated to the pig farmers of lowland Devon with waxwork pigs and hands-on exhibitions on how to fatten pigs yet leave them

25

happy and content. Or something like that. This afternoon your Mum has invited me to Sidmouth to see the latest exhibitions of flower-arranging, this time built around a cricket theme by the WI members there. Or something like that." Michael replied, feeling that his life was set to repeat. "Do you want to join me in Sidmouth later?"

"Pass. Meeting with publisher today, we are lunching at the Royal Lion[7]. Had you forgotten?" Judy said, giving Michael a look which was meant to convey, 'Are you so jealous of my career that you pay no heed to what I do within it or say about it?' It was of course lost on him.

"Sorry, Jude. I had forgotten. I can put your mother off and dash back from the historical delights or otherwise of pig-farming and join you."

"No, it's okay my reviewing hero. You stick to your plan. It's a business lunch, dry (as the wine may be) and not very exciting."

"And you don't want me there," he said and instantly wished he hadn't, but not instantly enough.

The slam of the door and a shout of 'goodbye' from Annabelle and a grunt from Katy signified the girls' departure for school. Another slam of another door signified Judy's retreat into her study. A slam of the back door signified Michael's frustration with himself. How did he ever get to be this stupid? How did he get to stop being this stupid?

---

[7] Built in 1601 as a coaching inn, the Hotel has been extensively refurbished, yet still retains much of its history and unique charm.

26

Michael had returned to reviewing some months previously, in a small way at first covering local events for both the *Lyme Regis News* and *The View From Lyme*. His first review was of a revue presented by the Lyme Regis Strolling Players. Any thoughts he had that this would be a stroll in the park were very quickly dispelled. He wanted to be truthful; he wanted to tell it how it was. But how could he upset those lovely people who gave up their precious (or otherwise) time to entertain (after a fashion) their families, friends and paying customers? A liberal use of the word enthusiasm covered a multitude of performing sins. A liberal use of the word dedicated covered a woeful (at times) lack of technique. When he was stopped in the street and told, 'lovely review, Michael,' then he knew he had pitched it just right.

Being the former editor of *The Big Brash Guide to London* counted for nothing at the offices of *Devon World*. Philip 'call me Tim' Lucas had heard of Stephen 'call me Jim' Bailey, former editor of *The Big Brash Guide to London* whose demise under the wheels of a No. 59 bus had hastened Michael's editorship, but he had never heard of Michael. It was the Cotswolds all over again, it was shades of the *Cheltenham Post* and *Oxon Folk*.

"You'll have to prove yourself, Michael. For all I know, you are a reviewing lame duck."

Michael assured him he wasn't.

"What you did in London counts for nothing in Devon. This is a whole different kettle of reviewing."

Michael assured him he knew that. He was taken on. He proved to be no reviewing lame duck. He had never had been and hopefully never would be.

Judy's first two novels sold fairly well, indeed the second made the lower reaches of the national best-selling list. Encouraged by this success she had once again given up the tortures of being a teaching assistant, this time never to return. The third novel, *'The Game's Afoot'* (the title suggested to her by her publisher who wanted to go for a share of the Sherlock Holmes[8] market) was in the throes of publication and advance sales seemed to indicate the market was surprisingly buoyant for a combination of tennis and espionage. Judy had made a start on the fourth in the series, *'The Wimbledon Enigma'* a tale of code-breakers, murder, tennis, torture and strawberries and cream. It was going very well; it could even be game, set and match for this particular title. There was a blot on the horizon however and that particular blot chose that moment to knock on her study door (he knew better than to just walk in).

"Sorry, Jude," he said, sincerely yet hesitantly. Michael didn't always find apologising easy.

Judy found accepting apologies easy and she did just that.

"You silly man, there's no need to be jealous you know. You are brilliant at what you do. You were the best in London and you are now the best in Devon. Everyone says so. I just got lucky writing the rubbish I do, but I love it just as much as you love doing what you do."

"But it's not rubbish. I like what you do and how you do it. It's not jealousy, it's the realisation that I will never be able to write that novel I wanted to. It's the realisation that my father, unknown to me, was a more gifted writer than I could ever be. Call it

---

[8] No idea.

28

disappointment in myself, call it my failing, but don't ever call it a lack of pride in you. I am very proud of you."

"Thank you, Mike. I am of you too. You are going to be and make a success of whatever you do."

"Thank you."

"What time do you have to go out to your piggy museum?"

"About an hour I guess."

Judy folded her laptop and put it to one side.

"An hour eh? Let's go into the bedroom and discuss the passage of time shall we?" throwing Michael a look, which wonder of wonders he was able to decipher correctly.

"I like the way your mind works," he replied, following her.

** THE SURREY SEVEN**

The Surrey Seven, formed in 1965, is available at reasonable cost and is guaranteed to raise a smile at all your functions. Specialising in wedding receptions, anniversary parties and birthday parties.

Our never-changing repertoire capturing the music of six decades means there is musical enjoyment for all and remember…at a reasonable cost!

The combo is fronted by Hampshire born Eddie Fox who has been a part of the Surrey music scene for decades. He was once voted Hook's finest singer and in his stellar career has played on the same shows as such performers as the Dave Clark Five and Dave Dee, Dozy, Beaky, Mick and Titch.

He has gathered around him some of Surrey's oldest musicians, household names like; Derek 'Buddy' Valentine, Richard 'Dicky' Ruskin and Nigel 'Speedy' Trellis.

'Come and stamp your feet…

…to the Surrey Seven's beat.'

Contact: Eddie Fox on 01256 54321.

Chapter Four-A Retirement Party

Tom Kennedy, formerly something big in the city and more recently something big in floristry was thinking of the success and renown that floristry had brought him; his designs after all were sought after from Muswell Hill to East Grinstead, from Slough to Gravesend. Kennedy's Blooms-Ikebana Specialists was the florist to go to if artistic elegance was required. Everyone said so.

He was also thinking that it was time to turn his back on this blooming, budding business of his and find some time for both himself and Elspeth. Elspeth in fact was already as close to retirement as it could get. She still did her one day a week in the antique shop in East Molesey. Her involvement in the Molesey WI was as close to minimal as it could get. Her flower-arranging was still reckoned to have lost its lustre and spirit of adventure. Her jam was still reckoned to have lost a little of its flavour and *its* spirit of adventure. Her Victoria sponges still seldom rose to the occasion. A fresh start was needed. But where?

Tom suggested Bognor Regis. Elspeth's response was a regal, 'Bugger Bognor'[9]. Elspeth suggested Eastbourne. Tom's response

---

[9] Supposedly the last words of King George V when his physician suggested he might recover enough to visit the town.

was less than enthusiastic. Tom suggested Blackpool. Elspeth laughed, but not *too* unkindly. Elspeth suggested Sidmouth. Tom pondered. Nice looking town. Cricket club too. Folk festival[10] (well, okay that was the downside). Good pubs. Elspeth pondered. Fresh sea air. Close to Judy and the children. Oh and Michael. Thriving WI. Their ponderings were combined resulting in an overwhelming vote of (hopefully not misplaced) confidence in Sidmouth as retirement town of choice.

There had to be a farewell bash. But where? Molesey boat club was discounted. Bastards. Molesey cricket club was discounted. Bastards. The Pint and Parrot in Ember Lane had a function room which was known to function very well. Caterers were contacted and hired with the help of Fay, to ensure all their guests were well catered for.

There should be music of course. The guests would expect it. In a display of perversity or perhaps a rush of blood to the head, Tom and Elspeth elected to hire the Surrey Seven who were still ploughing their own inimitable musical furrow, adopting and adapting all musical styles that had appeared since their inception in 1965 and creating their own inimitable (very) style. The Surrey Seven were now the Surrey Six following the death of Derek 'Buddy' Valentine (real name Brown) who had passed away at his drum kit while attempting a particularly difficult backward fill. Eddie Fox, erstwhile leader of the combo (still trading on his reputation as Hook's finest vocalist even though that particular

---

[10] There has been a folk festival in Sidmouth in the first week of August every year since 1955, attracting tens of thousands of visitors to over 700 diverse events with a promise of 'something for everyone'.

honour was awarded by the readers of the *Hook Gazette* as long ago as 1967) had decided that Derek was irreplaceable by another drummer despite the entreaties of Bill 'Jelly Roll' Morton, otherwise known as 'the mad stick man of Chobham', who maintained that he could bring a steady beat and rhythm hitherto unknown to the band. In fact, Eddie replaced Derek Valentine with a fully programmable drum machine which the band affectionately named 'Buddy'.

Fay, Tom and Elspeth's elder daughter, who was now something big in the city herself, had organised the catering. She was the best man/woman for the job. Everyone said so.

She was now the acting Chief Executive of the British arm of Stammersson Inc, a company specialising in Norwegian furniture and accessories for the home with an appealing (very) Scandinavian (very) twist. She spent three to four months of the year in Fredrikstad, where the company was based in an ultra-modern building off Mosseveien, which rivalled for style the nearby buildings of Østfold University College. Home there, was a rented bungalow (paid for by Stammersson) surrounded by a manicured lawn and mature trees (Norwegian wood-could be a song that) in Merkuleven. There she could have entertained her Norwegian lovers if she had any, cooked up splendid meals (heavy on fish) for her Norwegian friends if she had any. Instead, she slept and ate by herself after long days in the office planning new sales campaigns, after long days in the factory in Sellebakk examining and praising new products that would go down a storm in the United Kingdom, where her house in Weybridge was remarkably free not just of Norwegian furniture or accessories with a Scandinavian twist, but also boyfriends, Norwegian or any other nationality.

The catering company that Fay had sourced (Fiennes Fine Dining) had provided many a corporate dinner for Stammersson Inc and had done so with a certain amount of aplomb, winning praise from all quarters for their variations on British food, their various takes on European fine dining and their fresh approach to giving businessmen and women exactly what they wanted or thought they wanted. They also had a novel approach to the fees they charged 'the more you pay the less you get' was their motto and at least one of those truisms was always adhered to. Fortunately for Tom, Fay had offered to pay for all the food and drink.

The Fiennes team, led by Steve Newsome, voiced some disquiet about the cramped area that manfully doubled as a kitchen in The Pint and Parrot, but Fay suggested to Steve that he look on it as a challenge. It was pretty much what she had said to him about herself a few months previously. He had risen to that challenge three days afterwards and continued to rise to the challenge throughout their five month long affair conducted in hotels scattered throughout London and the Home Counties.

"Mr Kennedy, may I have a word?" asked Eddie Fox, Hook's finest vocalist.

"Yes of course," said Tom, who was hoping he would not be asked about his musical preferences, he had never been something big where music was concerned.

"It's about Dicky."

"Dicky?" queried a puzzled Tom.

"You know him better as Richard Ruskin our saxophonist."

"Ah," said Tom, who knew the aforementioned Richard Ruskin not at all, let alone better.

"You may remember his little kazoo solo on the occasion of your daughter's wedding as you both danced to 'Isn't She Lovely'. It was a memorable moment I'm sure you'll agree."

Tom certainly agreed that one of those moments was memorable, he was none too sure of the other.

"Anyway, Dicky has had a few problems this week, palpitations, chest pains and shortness of breath. So I'm just tipping the wink to you that he may be off his game and we may have to rein ourselves in to accommodate him as it were. I trust you'll make allowances."

"I already had."

"Had what?"

"Made allowances for the band having an off day."

"But how could you, Mr Kennedy? I have only just told you."

"I...er...if you will excuse me I have to greet some guests," said Tom, pirouetting away in a move worthy of any dance floor.

The guests in question were Michael, Judy, Katy and Annabelle.

"Is Fay here, dad?"

"In the kitchen with Steve of Fiennes, the caterers. They seem to be getting on very well. Perhaps something will come of it."

"Oh, dad."

"What?"

"Hello girls, you've brought your dad with you then," said Elspeth, who had been assisting the band with a sound check, not that they needed one in her opinion…for any reason.

"He gets grumpy if we leave him behind," replied Annabelle.

"Grumpier," asserted Katy, asserting herself.

"Where's Judy?" asked Elspeth.

"With Fay," answered Tom.

"And where is Fay? Don't say with Judy!"

"With Steve Newsome of the caterers, in the kitchen. I was just saying," said Tom, "that she gets on well with this Steve and perhaps something will come of it."

"Oh, Tom."

"What?"

Tom shot a look at Michael which was meant to convey 'do you know what that was about'. Michael shot a look at Tom which conveyed to Tom only too well that Michael didn't have a clue about either Tom's look or the situation. Elspeth, Fay and Judy returned from the cramped area manfully doubling as a kitchen exchanging knowing looks. 'Are we becoming a nation of mime artists?' thought Michael.

"Have you planned your speech, Tom?"

"A speech, Michael?"

"It's expected on occasions like this. Your speech at the wedding went down…"

"Like a lead balloon I know."

"No, it went down well, Tom. If you put your mind to it you could be something big in after dinner speaking," said Michael, with some sincerity, but only a little.

Katy and Annabelle were attacking the sandwiches with a relish. Car journeys coupled with their dad's driving and navigational skills always left them either hungry, tired or both. Steve Newsome watched them with some trepidation and a touch of annoyance; Fiennes Fine Dining was not used to children attacking sandwiches with or without relish. On the other hand, they were Fay's nieces. Be nice to her nieces and she would continue to be nice to him. He was fully conversant with the niceties of life.

The Surrey Seven/Six featuring 'Buddy' the drum machine launched into their never-changing repertoire. Eddie Fox, Hook's finest, brought the sound of skiffle to The Pint and Parrot insisting, with a glaring lack of conviction, that his old man was a dustman.[11] Tom Kennedy, who had never been something big in waste collection failed to see the relevance of the song. But he was not alone in questioning the relevance of songs in The Surrey Seven/Six featuring Buddy the drum machine's never-changing repertoire through the years.

---

[11] "My Old Man's a Dustman" is a song first recorded by the British skiffle singer Lonnie Donegan. It reached number one in the British, Australian, Canadian and New Zealand singles charts in 1960.

At least their next number had a kind of relevance for Tom as they re-worked The Move's 'Flowers in the Rain'[12] minus the opening thunderstorm effect. Eddie Fox's spoken, 'imagine a thunderstorm raging' did not quite work. Everyone said so. It was though, a spirited performance, but the one of the many things you could say about Eddie Fox was that he was far from being Roy Wood.[13] Not that he was alone in that, there were many people who were not Roy Wood.

Gary the barman came through to the function room in search of Tom. He was successful.

"There are a couple of geezers in the bar who wanted me to ask you whether they would be welcome to come in. They said they had olive branches for you although it don't look like they have brought anything, mate."

"Would these…er…geezers be Nigel Boycott from the boat club and Tim James from the cricket club?"

"Dunno, what am I, a mind-reader? But one of them called the other Tim. Come to think of it he called the other one Nige."

This was an unexpected turn of events. Nigel and Tim had been the prime movers behind Tom being expelled from their respective clubs when he was under suspicion of all manner of illegal financial manoeuvres. True, they had offered olive branches before, but these had been swiftly rejected by Tom. A few years had

---

[12] The first record to be played on Radio One.

[13] Lead singer of The Move, founder of Wizzard and co-founder of ELO.

38

gone by now and Tom was no longer as bitter as he had been. He had moved on, he had taken the opportunities that had come his way to forge another career. And now as he was preparing to take his leave of Surrey, surely he could afford to be magnanimous.

"I have a one word answer for them, Gary."

"Is it no?"

"Yes."

"It's yes?"

"No, it's no."

"No?"

"Yes."

Gary, baffled by this exchange stood his ground, failing utterly to interpret what was required of him. Tom, sensing Gary's bewilderment, changed his one word answer to another one word answer.

"Gary, tell them Tom says, 'bastards'."

Gary, no longer baffled, merely puzzled went off to deliver Tom's stinging message and Tom resumed his mingling not that he had ever been something big in mingling. Before he could mingle further Elspeth collected him and escorted him to the dance floor where, until that moment, any form of dancing had been conspicuous by its absence.

Judy shot Michael a look which was meant to convey 'shall we join them?' Judy understood Michael's blank look only too well and taking the bull and her husband by the horns dragged him onto the dance floor to the embarrassment of Katy and Annabelle who had already decided they had never heard music like this in their lives. Sentiments which may well have been echoed throughout the function room.

The Surrey Seven/Six featuring 'Buddy' the drum machine, encouraged by this move elected to launch into their highly individual rendition of 'We Are Family[14]'. It was a rendition that left everything to the imagination of the beholders. One of the many things you could say about Eddie Fox was that he was far from being Kathy Sledge,[15] not that he was alone in that, there were many people who were not Kathy Sledge. The nifty guitar riff of the original was performed in a perfunctory fashion by 'Nigel 'Speedy' Trellis acknowledged by one and all as Surrey's answer to Bert Weedon[16] although that was entirely dependent on the question being posed.

"Odd isn't it," observed Michael whilst allowing Judy to lead him around the dance floor. His dodgy knees precluded his taking the lead in many activities, dancing in particular. And he didn't always find public displays of rhythm easy.

---

[14] A massive hit for Sister Sledge.

[15] Kathy, one of the four sisters, was 16 years old at the time of recording.

[16] Herbert Maurice William 'Bert' Weedon, OBE (10 May 1920 – 20 April 2012) was an English guitarist whose style of guitar playing was popular and influential during the 1950s and 1960s.

"I think I need a bit more of a clue than that," replied a leading Judy, who was concentrating on avoiding Michael's dodgy knees.

"Eddie Fox. Or Kathy Sledge as he is now."

"Has the dancing gone to your head? What are you talking about?"

"Listen to me Jude. Eddie Fox. Captain Edward de Vere Fox."

"Ah."

"Ah? Is that it?"

"I think ah sums it up perfectly. Look, it's coincidence. But if not, just march up to Eddie and tell him that you think his dead great great great and one more great for luck grandfather is dead and well in our garden. Perhaps you can request a song at the same time. How about, 'There's a Ghost in my House?'[17]

"I just thought it was odd that's all."

"Coincidence," said Judy firmly as 'We Are Family' came to a merciful end.

Katy came across to them. "Do you have to do that?"

"We were only dancing, Katy!" said Michael.

"That's what I meant…it's gross. You wouldn't catch me dancing to that old stuff."

"Katy!"

---

[17] A hit for R. Dean Taylor.

"Hi Gramps, okay?"

"I will be when you have danced with your old granddad."

Katy shot her parents a look which could have laid waste to a small country and a look to her granddad which was meant to convey, 'I don't want to, I'd rather die, but I think I have to'. Judy recognised the look. The men didn't.

Tom launched Katy onto the floor just in time for the Surrey Seven/Six featuring Buddy the drum machine's highly individual take on Clive Dunn's[18] 'Grandad.'[19] The tuba of composer, Herbie Flowers[20] being replaced by Richard 'Dicky' Ruskin's tenor sax, which added nothing to the song because 'Dicky's' medical difficulties of the day, which echoed his medical diificulties of most days, rendered his saxophone almost inaudible. All the same, most folk considered that to be a saving grace. This could not be said for the malfunctioning 'Buddy' which halfway through the song replaced the gentle ¾ time signature of the original with a demented beat all of its own. The band tried to keep up, Tom and Katy tried to keep up, but to no avail, their best efforts were in vain. 'Buddy' won the day.

---

[18] A character actor in comedy best known for his role as Corporal Jack Jones in Dad's Army.

[19] Reached #1 in the UK charts.

[20] Best known for his contribution on bass to Lou Reed's 'Walk on the Wild Side'.

"Is there a programmer in the house?" asked Eddie Fox, who was now wishing that Bill 'Jelly Roll' 'mad stick man' Morton was on board.

There wasn't.

As the band searched through their never-changing repertoire for acoustic numbers which would not require the presence of 'Buddy', Tom and Elspeth decided that the unscheduled break had given them the perfect opportunity to say their official goodbyes. Hand in hand they stood on the spot that Eddie Fox had just vacated.

Elspeth stepped forward and The Surrey Seven/Six excluding the disgraced 'Buddy' improvised a quick (although not quick enough for some) burst of 'There's No One Quite Like Grandma'[21] which even St Winifred's School Choir would have found cringe worthy. Elspeth silenced them with a look. It was a look that Michael recognised as being *the* look, the one that he had come to expect from Judy on occasion.

"Let me first say I'm slightly confused by all these wonderful things people have been saying about us all evening. Not that we don't agree with your comments. In fact, I could add a few other qualities I think you have overlooked. But what genuinely confuses me is that none of you have bothered to mention these feelings to us before. If you'd only come and spoken to us before we retired, who knows, we might have stayed. Don't panic, just joking. We would have at least spoken a little more kindly of you. Even towards you,

---

[21] There's No One Quite Like Grandma was a number one hit single by Stockport-based primary school choir St Winifred's School Choir.

for that matter. Although we can give you no guarantees there can we, Tom?"

Tom indicated his agreement by shaking his head which momentarily confused Elspeth.

"I would like to add to Elspeth's comments and say thank you to all our friends and family for turning out. Are you sure you are not just wanting to make sure we are going? I told myself I would not get up in front of anybody ever again after my speech at Judy's wedding, yet here I am and this will be the last time unless there should be another wedding in the near future."

Everybody turned and looked at Fay.

"I have renewed hopes of that after today funnily enough."

Everybody turned and looked at Steve Newsome.

"Oh, Tom," said Elspeth.

"What?"

"Oh, dad," said Fay and Judy.

"What? Why is everyone saying oh, Tom or oh, dad to me?"

"Oh, Tom," said Elspeth.

"Oh, dad," said Judy.

Tom sat down, as bewildered and puzzled as Gary had been earlier. Tom, like Michael, didn't always find life easy. Elspeth sat down, leaving the band to do their thing, whatever it was. There were handshakes and smiles all round as the evening wore on. The music flowed almost as if it was music. And the conversations became louder. The jokes coarser. The children sleepier.

The band had long finished and was in the throes of packing up the equipment and putting 'Buddy' in the naughty box when Michael approached Hook's finest, Eddie Fox.

"May I have a word about your family?"

"My family? Is this about my brother, I'll have you know he was found not guilty. He had been dressed up like that by someone and then photographed. And as for the other matter, well, that could happen to anyone, don't you agree?"

"Well, quite…and he…what…er…anyway I had more distant family members in mind. Do you know if any of your ancestors fought in the civil war?"

"I could draw up a chart for you. We were known for our soldiers. Killing is very much a family tradition."

"Is it? Splendid," not that Michael thought it was in any way splendid. "Thank you, but I don't think a chart will be necessary. Does the name Edward de Vere Fox mean anything to you?"

"Yes it does. A brave man who laid down his life in deepest Dorset fighting for Cromwell[22] and Parliament. A captain you know. All our soldiers were officers. He is revered within our family as one of our greatest sons. Why do you ask?"

---

[22] Oliver Cromwell (25 April 1599 – 3 September 1658) was an English military and political leader and later Lord Protector of the Commonwealth of England, Scotland and Ireland.

"It's nothing really. Thank you," Michael replied. Well, he couldn't tell him, could he? Not really.

"We were a family of soldiers, barristers, taxidermists, but only one solitary singer!" Eddie said, laughing.

"Oh, who was that?" Michael asked and instantly wished he hadn't, but not instantly enough. The man had done (almost) nothing to merit such sarcasm.

Eddie's look, one that he could decipher, shamed him all the way back to his family.

Chapter Five-Present Day

After their brief yet pleasurable discussion regarding the passage of time Michael and Judy went their separate ways. Judy retreated to her study to try and find the plot that she had unaccountably misplaced somewhere in chapter five of *The Wimbledon Enigma*. She now had two hours spare in which to find it before her lunch at the Royal Lion.

Michael was on his way to the new museum which was housed in a former piggery (what else?) between Exeter and Crediton. With luck he could be in and out fairly quickly and on his way to Sidmouth. With luck, a quick pint with Tom in the Black Horse and then wander up to the old United Reform chapel where the Sidmouth WI practiced their flower-arranging and black arts.

He had arranged to meet the curate of the museum, Susan Jones at 10.15 sharp. He arrived at 10.41. Michael didn't always find navigating easy, something his family would readily testify to. His lack of punctuality had never been in doubt. He was always late. He had expected the museum to be of the hands-on type that were all the rage, but had not expected it to be feet-on so was somewhat surprised to be handed a pair of wellington boots on arrival.

"We have a state of the art layout here demonstrating just how pig-farming got its start in Devon and how it prospered and grew throughout the centuries."

"And we need wellies for that do we?"

"Yes we do indeed, Mr Hamilton. We have the very finest synthetic mud to wade through representing exactly how the individual sties would have appeared. Technology has created for us the foodstuffs through the ages, from the waste products to the grains and vitamin-enriched foods of today. There is realism here," she said, proudly, but ironically.

"Has technology also come up with a synthetic material for the pig's own waste product?" he asked, fearing the worst.

"Yes and not just that. Look," she said, as they exited the rear of the museum.

Michael wasn't sure how impressed he was supposed to look or indeed to be, considerably more so then he was feeling no doubt. But he looked all the same. He was good like that.

"Do you see those beautiful pigs?"

He did. A country upbringing worked wonders in the recognition of pigs, beautiful or otherwise. He knew a pig when he saw it. Or in this case didn't.

"They are of course not real pigs."

"Of course, obviously not," Michael replied, although at first glance it was anything, but obvious.

"Cyber-pigs, robot-pigs, call them what you will, but are they not so beautiful, so life-like?"

Michael having mistaken them for the real thing could only agree that they were indeed life-like. He drew the line at calling them beautiful. He didn't always find praising livestock easy.

"So, we have synthetic food, synthetic mud, synthetic sh...er...waste products and synthetic pigs, but why not real pigs in real sties living their real lives for parents and children to wonder at? Is a thing only of any worth because technology has provided it? Would the stench of real pigs contaminate your no doubt multi-million pound museum? Is all this something you are proud of? A pig farm theme park with no pigs?" Michael expounded and instantly wished he hadn't, but not instantly enough. This woman had done (almost) nothing to merit his sarcasm. Some things however, needed saying.

The rest of his visit to the museum was uneventful and mostly conducted by Susan Jones in silence. A frosty silence. And unsurprisingly, it came to an end rather swiftly. It would be a relief to slip into the gentle world of flower arranging in Sidmouth.

Elspeth was already at the United Reform chapel where the Sidmouth WI met, by the time Michael arrived at the Kennedy's Coburg Terrace home.[23] He had thoughtfully rung when leaving the museum to say he would be with them easily by two o' clock. Rather less thoughtfully, he arrived at twenty one minutes past two. Parking the car proved challenging and after three attempts he left the vehicle encroaching a full three inches into the next door

---

[23] A delightful terrace overlooking the tennis courts.

49

neighbour's allocated parking space. Michael had never found parallel parking easy.

Miss Smollett, for it was she, had observed this manoeuvre from behind her net curtains and was ready for a showdown, indeed she was always ready for a showdown; she protected her parking space with a passion. Not that she had a car. Or even drove. She had spent the last sixty-six years in a state of embitterment ever since Reginald Plympkin, a trainee solicitor, had jilted her at the altar of St Ignatius's in Frimley Green in 1953. Even worse than this, Reginald had, unknown to her, been carrying on with her best friend and fellow typist, Joan Prentice and within a few short weeks they had wed in Godalming. Since then she had mistrusted men with a vengeance. Truth be known she mistrusted everyone. In spite of the fierce competition in the town for the title, she had become Sidmouth's very own Miss Havisham.[24]

"How long do you intend to stay there, young man?" she shouted through the two inches of open window she allowed herself.

"I won't be long," Michael replied with a smile which he wrongly thought would win her over.

"You had better not be or you can be certain I will be taking steps, I can assure you of that." she warned as she retreated behind the safety of her curtains.

---

[24] Miss Havisham is a significant character in the Charles Dickens novel *Great Expectations* (1861). She is a wealthy spinster who lives in her ruined mansion with her adopted daughter, Estella. Dickens describes her as looking like "the witch of the place."

"What kind of steps does she think she can take?" asked Michael as he greeted Tom on the doorstep.

"My best guess would be that she is knitting a wheel clamp as we speak!"

****

Meanwhile…at the Royal Lion in Lyme Regis, Judy was polishing off a crème brulee which had been preceded by a main course of mushroom stroganoff. Connor Milligan, her publisher and Al Faraday her editor had spent the entire lunch tempting Judy with the prospect of lucrative book tours to many far-flung places (no, not Chipping Norton) and signings at prestigious book shops throughout the country and not just this country either. More television work was a carrot they also dangled. The benefits would be enormous they pointed out. The rewards high. The money unstoppable. Income tripled at least. Fame, Judy, fame.

Judy was on the point of giving her well-rehearsed answers when there came a beep:

Wat time is dinner?

Around six and it's what, not wat, Katy.

Grrr. I wanna go out early.

Sorry, Katy, you can't and it's want to not wanna.

O GR8 lifes so unfair.

It's oh not o, great not GR8 and don't forget your apostrophes. x

Beep. "Sorry, guys."

Judy, have u heard from Michael? He is twenty minutes late. X

Twenty minutes is not late, dad, not for Mike. And it's you not u. x

I was trying to be cool hip and modern Judy LOL x

Be yourself. You are never going to be something big in text speak.

Beep. "Sorry, guys."

Hey Jude, how is the lunch going? What have they talked you into?

Nothing because people keep texting me!!! X

Silence. More silence. She tapped out a message.

Sorry Mike, that wasn't aimed at you. Love you. X

Good. Luv u 2 x

It's love you too or maybe also. X

I no!

Aaaarrggghhh. Go away xxx

Beep.

Hold on. What's not me?

Oh, Dad I meant it's not u it's you! X

"Just think, Judy if you were on a book signing tour, you could get away from all that."

"All what, Connor?"

"Family stuff," replied Connor, whose only family was a Persian cat named Teazel and a cousin named Nigel in Wath upon Dearne.

"I have no wish to get away from 'family stuff' as you call it. If I am away from them for one day it's a day too long. I do my bit, Connor and the books are doing well after all."

Judy had definitely done her bit. Everyone said so. She had given interviews to national dailies, she had allowed herself to be featured in various trade magazines, had even appeared on television in *Books for All* and the quiz show, *Chapter and Verse or Worse*. She had turned down an invitation to take part in the new reality shows; *I'm a Writer...Get Me In The Library* and *Writing On Ice*. There had been book signings throughout the south-west, the Home Counties and London. Yes, she had definitely done her bit.

"I don't dispute that, Judy, but there are vast opportunities out there. You could be big in the States and then, who knows, Hollywood may come calling."

"Already has actually."

"Really?" asked an apoplectic Connor Milligan, hands shaking as they reached out for the wine.

"Yes, Holly Wood, she's a mobile hairdresser from Hawkchurch, came round yesterday. I can recommend her and her sister, Pine Wood."

"Very funny," said Al Faraday who actually found it anything but funny. But then, he found few things funny. "Why do you treat everything as a joke?"

"Mostly because it is. I'm a mother first and foremost, I am a wife secondly. Being a writer comes way after that. I am not a star, I am not a celebrity and I'm sorry, Connor, I cannot increase my level of involvement in marketing because my level of involvement with Michael, Katy and Annabelle takes priority. I'm grateful, of course I am and I'm sure we can work well together for many years to come, but don't ask too much of me."

Connor Milligan knew better than to argue with Judy Hamilton. She had enabled him to become a big fish in the publishing world. Not to put too fine a point on it, she may well make his fortune as well as her own. Plans were afoot to translate the books into French, Italian, Russian, Spanish and German (but not Klingon, Judy was pleased to observe). And that was just the tip of the language iceberg. So he would indeed be careful not to ask too much of her. It didn't stop him hoping though or even scheming.

****

"I suspect your involvement in this flower-arranging event, Tom," observed Michael as they sipped their pints in the Black Horse.

"I may have given them one or two pointers. Elspeth really wants this to be a success especially after the debacle of the 'Basque Night'."

They fell silent, both reflecting on the debacle of the 'Basque Night'.

"Easy mistake to make after all," said Tom.

"Yes, anyone could have made it. Well, not anyone maybe, but..."

"Quite. Mind you, it could have been worse."

"I suppose so. Well, actually, *could* it have been any worse?"

"No, not really," said Tom with a solemn shake of the head, but a grin as wide as the esplanade.

The United Reform chapel was already full when Michael and Tom eventually turned up. It was a charity event to raise funds for the Distressed Wives of Devon Cricketers. The various floral arrangements were built around cricket themes, obviously not an easy thing to accomplish observed Michael, as each arrangement looked identical to his untrained in floristry eye. The only nod to cricket being in the name of each one; googly, long leg, silly mid-on etc. His attention wandered to a section of the wall covered in photographs. All were of various dishes. There were a few blanks spaces in the display; he had a good idea what these blank spaces may have contained. Still, it wouldn't hurt to have confirmation.

"Good turnout, Elspeth, I'm very impressed with the level of expertise shown in the displays. These pictures on the wall though, what are they of?"

"The 'Basque Night', but I'm sure you knew that."

"There appears to be some pictures missing, what were they of?"

"Of me, but I'm sure you knew that," she said, coldly and walked off.

What was the matter with him, making fun of his mother in law? She had done (almost) nothing to merit his teasing. A walk of shame across the tiled chapel floor. An apology offered. An apology accepted.

The chairwoman of DWODC, Elaine Huxtable accosted him and gave him the run down on DWODC's aims. She was of the opinion that Michael may view the group as frivolous or flippant. Full marks for her perception because that's exactly how he viewed the group. She was further of the opinion that Michael could not possibly consider them a worthy cause. Bulls-eye again. Elaine had a captive audience, one she was not about to relinquish without a fight. Over the following few minutes she force-fed Michael tales of charitable works; of mowers bought, of squares re-laid, of cookers being replaced. The 'distressed' he was informed was meant ironically for the 'wives' loved their cricket as much as their husbands and partners. Elaine's own husband, Brian was a wicket-keeper of some note, revered for his glove work from Topsham to Totnes. Her lover, Graham Jackman was inordinately proud of his googlies and his follow through was a thing of wonder, everyone said so. All in all, Elaine was far from being a distressed wife although unknown to him, Brian teetered on the edge of being a distressed husband. Elaine stated her case and cause with simple clarity and although Michael felt somewhat badgered, he would come up with a piece perfectly in keeping with the occasion. He was good like that.

Michael reminded Tom and Elspeth that they would be visiting them in two Sunday's time. Tom and Elspeth reminded Michael that they would be seeing Michael and Judy in a couple of day's time for Katy's birthday and wondered how Michael could have forgotten. It didn't occur to them that perhaps Judy had forgotten. Not that she had. Nor had Michael to be perfectly honest, he had just passed on the message he had been given. He was good like that. Michael didn't always find remembering birthdays easy, but there was a limit, even for him.

****

Michael had only just now, on this balmy early summer evening, thought to apprise Captain Edward de Vere Fox regarding his descendant. The captain had taken the news of the fifty year career of his family member and namesake reasonably well. The bluff soldier he had once been had been replaced by a more pragmatic persona as befits three hundred and eighty-five years of life and death and life. (It's complicated.)

"A balladeer, Michael? I can scarcely believe it, but I suppose that times do change and families with it. But, all that tradition of soldiering, butchering and killing. I mean, why would anyone want to give all that up?"

Michael had a very good idea why, but didn't want to disenchant the captain further. He did try to assuage the captain's feelings by telling him that he had personally heard Eddie Fox singing 'You're In The Army Now'[25] and 'Soldier Of Fortune'[26] although neither song had any great relevance to the wedding reception and retirement party they had been offered up to. Perhaps

---

[25] A hit for Status Quo in 1986.

[26] A song on Deep Purple's 1974 Stormbringer album.

understandably, this did not raise the captain's spirit and he faded away in the direction of the stream with several shakes of his head.

And now our newly materialised gallant captain was being browbeaten by Katy regarding her rights as she leapt into her teenage years. It was not a subject he could claim to have any special knowledge or insight into. He had been married yes, in the spring of 1628 to Elizabeth Weaver of Aldershot. She, however, bore him only one child and rather a surprising amount of ill-will. Irish Meg, when called for, was largely sympathetic, but did nothing to aid Katy's cause when she said that she was married at thirteen and bore the first of her fourteen children at fourteen.

"Katy, come on in please, dinner is ready," shouted Michael.

"In a minute!"

"Now, if you please. Let the captain and Irish Meg get back to…well…whatever it is they want to do."

"Life's so unfair," grumbled Katy as she entered the *spacious* and *fully modernised* kitchen. "I thought the captain would be on my side at least."

"Perhaps he feels diplomacy is the best course," her dad said, who knew about these things, allegedly.

"Perhaps he just can't be bothered to help you as you have turned so nasty recently," said Annabelle, entering the fray, unwisely as her shins were well in reach of Katy's left foot which recently had been displaying an accuracy that Johnny Norfolk would have been proud of.

"Girls, girls," shouted Michael to no avail.

"Girls, girls," shouted Judy to a great deal of avail as she came into the room.

The girls stopped instantly.

"Hey Jude, how do you do that?"

"Naturally gifted, I guess!"

The dinner was a slight affair, chiefly consisting of salad, Michael and Judy both having lunched reasonably well. Katy thought this most unfair. Annabelle agreed with her, but was still careful to protect her shins. Agreeing with her sister counted for nothing these days.

Chapter Six-A Basque Night

Everyone agreed it wasn't really Elspeth's fault. After all, she had been ill. She had missed a couple of meetings. Then there was the fault with the heating in the chapel which meant another week had gone by. The news of the Basque Night was passed on second-hand or possibly third-hand to Elspeth. No, she could hardly be blamed under the circumstances.

At first, all seemed well. The tables joined end to end against the left wall were positively bursting with all the best culinary dishes of the Basque region as interpreted by members of the Sidmouth WI.

Gâteau Basque, Cuajada, Marmitako, Piperade, Txipirones and more, all lovingly prepared and presented chiefly by four members, none of whom had been to the Basque region. Mrs Wilbrahams, who *had* been to the Basque region and had delighted fellow members with tales (not lurid) of time spent in Bayonne[27] was

---

[27] In southwestern France, Bayonne is ideally situated for access to the Pyrenees Mountains and the Atlantic coast. The town, sitting on the confluence of the Nive and Adour rivers, boasts a wealth of gourmet traditions and events which reflect both its Basque and

unable to attend due to her husband's ingrowing toe-nail which rendered him practically helpless although in her opinion it was always thus.

Elspeth's error did not even register with her during the first ten minutes as she was otherwise engaged in discussing details of her recent illness for which she blamed Tom. Tom had recently recovered from a bout of man flu,[28] which he generously passed on to her. Her coat therefore stayed on. Although the chapel had an adequate heating system (in spite of its recent malfunction) which had been recently repaired, it had chosen this particular occasion to be rather slow to achieve its ultimate aim; that of heating the building. Therefore other coats stayed on.

Elspeth even studied the food on show without registering any alarm. When she felt sufficiently warm she duly took off her coat. If there had been any traffic in the room, which of course there wasn't, she would have stopped it dead. Other coats were removed to show a variety of dresses and cardigans (and a solitary striped t-shirt worn by Betty Jamieson, entering into the Basque spirit although she, like so many people, drew the line at a beret) rarely seen outside of Sidmouth. But only one basque was on show.

Everyone agreed the mesh and lace detail was very fetching indeed. Everyone agreed that Elspeth would have to be careful she did not catch her death of cold. Everyone agreed it was entirely

---

Gascon influences. Thousands of years of history and our art for living make Bayonne both a fun-filled and interesting place to stay.

[28] Recognised by the WHO as a major and crippling illness.

inappropriate, but that it definitely showed Elspeth in a new light. No one could agree whether it was a favourable light.

Elspeth would have rather not be shown in any kind of light. Her face turned a deep shade of purple which matched the basque perfectly. Everyone said so. Then an odd thing occurred. Elspeth seemed to revel in her notoriety; any embarrassment she felt was countermanded by being the centre of attention. This had not happened since 2010 when she masterminded the Molesey WI sponsored abseil down the south wall of the Houses of Parliament. She still considered it her defining moment within the WI in spite of the divided opinion and adverse publicity it garnered.

By the time she arrived home however, this triumph had turned into a Pyrrhic victory[29] of epic proportions. Far from believing her standing within the Sidmouth WI to be enhanced she now considered that she had fallen far in everyone's eyes, a figure of fun to be laughed at in the lounges and drawing-rooms (unlike many towns, Sidmouth still had many a drawing-room) of the town. And there were photographs. Miss Cecily Hawksmoor with her trusty yet old (very) Pentax had been doing the rounds, flashing away (although everyone agreed it was Elspeth doing the flashing). Perhaps she could be bought off. She had heard she was partial to lemon drizzle cake and Elspeth's lemon drizzle cakes were a thing of wonder. Everyone said so.

The one that she duly baked for Miss Cecily Hawksmoor was indeed a cake of wonder, a cake that would have bought anyone off. Feeling a little better about herself and her standing, she placed the

---

[29] A Pyrrhic victory is a victory with such a devastating cost that it is tantamount to defeat.

cake carefully in her very best cake tin. She had bought it in 1983 during a trip to Skegness (her holiday sights and sites were set lower then) but if Miss Hawksmoor took a shine to it then she could have it along with its contents. Miss Hawksmoor, however, had the temerity to be away; on holiday her neighbours said, somewhere exotic they believed (presumably not Skegness). Tom expressed his heartfelt thanks for Miss Hawksmoor's vacation plans as he made his way through the lemon drizzle cake later. Elspeth found she had no appetite at all.

As the next meeting approached, Elspeth through some rather nifty yet devious moves managed to have the key of the United Reform chapel in her possession. Miss Hawksmoor was back from her 'somewhere exotic' holiday (actually Torquay) and had been spotted by Elspeth in the High Street. She tailed her in a manner that Johnny Stevens would have been proud of (not that she had ever heard of him, few had outside of Michael's head) and when Miss Hawksmoor entered the chapel she had her man/woman. A surreptitious glance through the window (which puzzled Mrs Wilbrahams who was en route to Potbury's[30] to gaze at the new range of dining tables that she sadly could no longer afford) confirmed Elspeth's suspicions that Miss Hawksmoor's visit involved photographs and the positioning of. Now all Elspeth had to do was obtain a key. Which she did…

She discovered the following day that there were six photographs of her. Six too many. Ripping them off the notice board which manfully doubled as a gallery, she stuffed them in her handbag (not bought in Skegness) and as she strolled nonchalantly (hopefully) around the town she deposited fragments of her shame

---

[30] A well-established furniture and department store in Sidmouth.

in various litter bins. None have ever come to light. Even now, they probably lie undisturbed in a landfill site or a seagull's stomach.

Of course it was entirely possible Miss Hawksmoor may have the negatives, but then there could always be a further lemon drizzle cake and an invitation to tea perhaps where these matters could be discussed in a civil manner. Blackmail always seemed not quite so criminal an act when accompanied by tea and cake. Not that Elspeth was well versed in blackmail.

Of course questions were asked about the glaring gaps where the photographs had once been. There were a number of possibilities put forward. There was many a theory. No one came up with any answers, save for Elspeth and Miss Hawksmoor, who had proved surprisingly amenable to both Elspeth's suggestions and her lemon drizzle cake, but these answers they wisely kept to themselves.

LEMON DRIZZLE CAKE

Ingredients:

225g unsalted butter, softened

225g caster sugar

Four Eggs

One finely grated zest 1 lemon

225g self-raising flour

For the drizzle topping:

The juice of 1½ lemons

85g caster sugar

Method: Heat oven to 180C/fan 160C/gas 4. Beat together 225g softened unsalted butter and 225g caster sugar until pale and creamy and then add 4 eggs, one at a time, slowly mixing through. Sift in 225g flour, then add the finely grated zest of 1 lemon and mix until well combined. Line a loaf tin (8 x 21cm) with greaseproof paper, then spoon in the mixture and level the top with a spoon.

Bake for 45-50 mins. until a thin skewer inserted into the centre of the cake comes out clean. While the cake is cooling in its tin, mix together the juice of 1 1/2 lemons and 85g caster sugar to make the drizzle. Prick the warm cake all over with a skewer or fork and then pour over the drizzle – the juice will sink in and the sugar will form a lovely, crisp topping. Leave in the tin until completely cool, then remove and serve. Eat!! Enjoy!

GATEAU BASQUE

Makes 6 servings

Ingredients:

For almond pastry

- 8 3/4 ounces (250 g) all-purpose flour

- 4 1/2 ounces (125 g) sugar

- one 4 oz. stick (125 g) unsalted butter

- 1 ounce (25 g) almond flour

- 1/4 teaspoon almond extract

- 1 egg

- 1 teaspoon baking powder

- 1 lemon zest

- 1/2 orange zest

For pastry filling

- Cherry jam (Morello) Or pastry cream as below. But honestly, you have to use the jam!

Method:

In a bowl add flour, sugar, butter, baking powder, almond flour and lemon and orange zest. Mix until it looks like sand. Add the egg and the almond extract and mix until dough comes together, do not over mix. Wrap the dough in foil and let it rest in the freezer.

In the meantime prepare the pastry cream. Scrape the vanilla bean into the milk and bring to a boil. Whisk the egg yolks with the sugar until pale. Add the flour and whisk until incorporated. Temper the egg mixture by slowly adding half of the hot milk to it while whisking. Place the rest of the milk back on the heat until it starts boiling. Now whisk in the egg-milk-mixture and continue whisking for at least one minute to cook off the raw flour taste. Turn off the heat and spread the mixture out on a large surface in order for it to cool rapidly.

Preheat the oven to 375'F and grease an 8 inch (20 cm) cake pan or pastry dish. Cut the dough in half, and place one half back into the freezer. Roll out the other half to a circle of about 10 inches (25 cm) in diameter. Gently line the bottom and sides of the baking dish with the dough. Fill with either cooled pastry cream or cherry preserve.

Roll out the second half of the dough to about 8 inches (20 cm) in diameter. Carefully drape it over the cake filling and pinch together the edges of the two layers of dough to seal in the filling. Trim off any excess dough. Make a crisscross pattern on top and brush it evenly with an egg yolk diluted in a tiny bit of water. Bake it for 30 minutes or until golden brown.

Eat!!! Enjoy!!!!!

Chapter Seven-A Novel Approach

"Mike, do you remember that day two years ago?"

"I think you may need to be more precise than that!"

"I was going to be, obviously. It was the day you went to see the vicar, Timothy Norfolk (no relation) about the captain and his men."[31]

"Not that we knew about the captain then. Or his men. Or woman."

"Obviously. You left us on the beach if you recall and I was reading, yes?"

"Yes, is there a point to this?"

"Obviously. Am I saying obviously too much?"

"Obviously."

"Hah! Anyway, the book I was reading was set in the world of professional tennis with a smattering of espionage thrown in for good measure. Do you remember what you said to me about it?"

---

[31] See 'A Twist Of Lyme'. Please!

As it happened, Michael could. Not one of his best moments. One of those remarks that he instantly regretted, but not instantly enough.

"Yes, I do. I said that even you could write something like that."

"Well…I have. Or at least I have made a start."

"You have? When did this happen?"

"I started it a few weeks ago. I have thought long and hard about telling you. I know how much you have always wanted to write a novel yourself. You still can. I am not stealing your thunder."

"How could you? I have no thunder to steal, not now anyway."

Michael didn't always find playing second-fiddle easy.

"Come on, Mike. No sulking. You haven't read any of it yet…it may be rubbish."

"It probably will be," Michael said and regretted it instantly, but not instantly enough. He stumbled on, thinking an apology may only serve to exaggerate the insult. And taking it back an even more tacit confession it had been made at all. Michael didn't always find life easy, but this we know.

"Sorry, Jude. Call it surprise. I'm sure it will be very good indeed. Have you got a title yet?"

"*Game On.*"

"I like it; it's snappy and mercifully short."

"The novel may turn out to be mercifully short too!"

"Do I get to read some of it?"

"Of course. I haven't got very far, only to page *forty, love.*"

"Well done, Jude, that's *ace.*"

"Hah! You think you have an *advantage* now, do you?"

"It's not my *fault* I am so good at these wordplays."

"I am not at *break*ing *point* yet; I can still *rally.*"

"I wouldn't want to beat you anyway; you may get a *chip* on your shoulder."

"I don't know what the *deuce* you mean, Mike."

Michael, although he found wordplays themselves easy, didn't always find winning easy. Primarily because he never did. He conceded defeat in a last throw of the word playing dice.

"*Game, set and match* to you Jude."

"Thank you."

Judy fetched her laptop and opened up a section of '*Game On*' for scrutiny.

'He could sense the tension in the crowd. More than once, they had been reduced to a hush by the passages of play that unfurled before them. The rallies had been intense as they always were when he met Ross Tallin. How badly he wanted, no, needed to get off court, but his professional pride would brook no slacking off during those long, long rallies. Twenty-eight shots the last one although he had no idea, as ever, why he counted. Nearly all of them played from the baseline until the final flurry of shots at the net. He had seen Ross's drop shot coming and was waiting for it. His own lob was perfect, dropping onto the baseline just out of reach of the retreating Ross. One set all and the prospect of at least another ninety minutes to play at the very least. It was time he could ill afford. The rendezvous with Boris was fast approaching unless he had been betrayed or found out. He was as open with his tongue as he was with his cash. And there amongst the personnel of the trade delegation he was certain were goons who would be watching and waiting for any indiscretions of whatever nature. Boris had to be snaffled up, turned and bled dry of information while he still had information to give, while he still had a life to live. He had gained the man's trust, had seen what nuggets he could bring to the table. Boris's contacts within the Centre were such that everyone was tolerably confident that he would not be serving them up chicken feed. He was the real deal and a coup for the firm. And now, instead of sitting in a hotel room reeling Boris in, he was on a packed Centre Court thanks to the vagaries of the English summer and the re-arranged Wimbledon schedules. In the old days play would have been abandoned for the day and he would even now be welcoming Boris to the fold. But these days, Wimbledon's Centre Court had a roof and play had only been suspended for forty minutes, forty priceless minutes that could have enormous repercussions for the government, his well-being and his position within the firm.

He switched his attention back to the match and waited for Ross's serve to come booming down towards him. It was a dilemma. He was used to dilemmas, had learned through his years of training how to handle them, how to turn them to his advantage, but rarely were his dilemmas played out in front of fifteen thousand people plus a television audience of millions. Ross's serve passed him in a blur. He had sent it wide into the corner and the monitor read 237 km/h (147 mph). The blistering speed that Ross came up with on his serve tended to result in inaccuracies too. He was not overwhelmed by Ross's service, he knew all he had to do was bide his time. This brought him back to his dilemma. He had no time.'

"What do you think?"

"I think it's great, Jude. You've definitely got something there. I'm not at all sure what it is or who will want to read it and I don't mean that unkindly."

"Thanks. I agree with you, but who knows, there may be a market out there?!"

As it turned out, there was a market out there. Admittedly it took some finding. But Judy was fortunate to find a publisher who shared her optimism. The eighteen publishers who rejected her manuscript had shown no such optimism. Obviously.

Connor Milligan, a failed writer whose stories of an undertaker turned detective (Algernon Graves) had not engendered any optimism in anyone, let alone a publisher, had instead turned publisher himself. He did not specialise, but went for the scattergun approach of publishing absolutely anything and everything. It worked up to a point and he did find himself with the odd low-key success on his hands. And one or two odd, very odd writers as clients.

For instance, Cliff Armitage, whose novel of prospecting for gold in Mexborough was rightly panned by the critics. Shaun

Killarney, whose novel of romance among the sheep farmers of Bedfordshire was lambasted by one and all. Jack Gaynor whose novel which detailed the life of one family through their Sunday dinner get-togethers was roasted by the critics. Jenny Black, whose updated version of Snow White and the Seven Dwarfs, although belittled by some did find some favour. 'This is a skilled and heart-warming revamp of a much loved tale' was the fairest comment of them all.

Judy was as surprised as anyone to find herself with a real, bona-fide publisher although she had yet to learn of his scattergun approach. Michael, through his contacts, organised reviews in many magazines and journals. Reviews were as mixed as the mixed doubles match that Judy described in great detail at great length, but the positive comments outweighed the negative ones. Encouraged by this, Judy set to work on the next novel in the series, *Game Set and Match* which again featured Bradley Steel, international tennis player and government operative. To her surprise and to Connor's this book proved more popular than its predecessor. To give him his due, Connor was a dab hand when it came to garnering publicity and his assiduous use of the internet when it came to marketing proved a winner. *Game Set and Match* nudged into the Top 50 best sellers in the UK, sandwiched between two recipe books, neither of which involved the food of the Basque region.

There were marginal shifts in the household. Katy and Annabelle found that having a mother who wrote 'proper' books gave them a status that having a father who wrote reviews would and could never do. Judy, emboldened by the growing success she was achieving left the world of teaching and her Year 9 pupils to their own devices. Michael, feeling marginalised by the marginal shifts, returned to the world of reviewing. Tom, his father in law had once been something big in the city before becoming something big in floristry and now Michael was once more, as before, something big in reviewing, but for all that he was destined to be known as 'the husband of that writer'. And as we know, Michael didn't always find playing second-fiddle easy.

Chapter Eight-Present Day

Michael and Judy had been busy during the early hours of Saturday morning putting up banners and balloons to surprise Katy with. They had in fact been busy since seven o'clock although they questioned the necessity of this when Katy finally appeared at twelve-thirty.

"Happy Birthday, Katy!"

"Yeah, thanks," mumbled Katy, whose enthusiasm was affected by having to get up on a Saturday at this unearthly hour. She would have to post a comment on the TeenRights website and see what kind of feedback would result. Life being unfair would no doubt crop up often.

Annabelle, feeling virtuous because she had been up since ten-thirty, wished her sister a happy birthday, thrust a present and card into her hands and then retreated, being careful to keep her shins out of harm's and Katy's way.

Michael and Judy had deliberated long and hard over gifts. Michael in particular didn't find present buying easy. Whatever gadget they bought for her would be outdated by the time it had been unwrapped. When it came to music, they were none too sure what Katy actually listened to. True, they had heard noises from her room which could possibly be construed as music in a bass-heavy kind of way. Books were always a safe option, but they were none too sure what Katy read these days, possibly tales (not too lurid they hoped) of teen romances and vampire shape-shifters. They asked Annabelle. She didn't know. They settled on tokens, tokens for absolutely everything plus the mandatory smattering of bath accessories, gels and sprays. Katy seemed pleased. It was hard to tell.

The recently refurbished Three Cups[32] in Broad Street had a function room which functioned very well it was said and it was there that Katy's 13th Birthday party was taking place that evening. The room had panoramic views across the bay, but whether the assorted teenagers and near-teenagers would appreciate it was another matter entirely. The invitations had gone out to thirty-four girls and six boys. The six boys were unsure why they had been invited and even more unsure whether to accept. They did so only because they feared the fallout that a refusal would bring with it.

Michael was trying his hardest to persuade Katy to go and get dressed without a great deal of success. Judy took over, with a great deal of success.

"How do you do that?" was Michael's plea.

"Trade secret, Mike. Mum and Dad will be here soon so where do you fancy for lunch?"

---

[32] At time of writing the Three Cups on Lyme's Broad Street is empty and unused as it has been sadly for over twenty years,

"The Harbour Inn, if we can get in," offered Mike as he turned towards the window. "You'll never guess who is coming down the drive, Jude."

"Henry Kissinger?"

"Hah! It's Fay!"

"My sister, Fay?"

"No, Fay Weldon. Yes, of course your sister!"

The six years spent in Lyme Regis had been an entirely Fay-free zone. Fay always blamed pressures of work and her (at times) very active social life for the fact she had never visited. There had been many invitations; indeed there was an open invitation which had remained permanently closed from Fay's standpoint. Until now.

Michael was inclined to think there was a residue of the sibling rivalry that had blighted so much of the sisters' early lives. Judy took the view that Fay, although successful (very) in her field was maybe just a tad envious of the life that Judy had with Michael and the girls. Maybe, just maybe, it was the life she had imagined for herself. Neither Michael or Judy were particularly brave enough to broach these thoughts with Fay however.

"My God, Fay," screamed Judy, as she practically tore the car door off. "What on earth are you doing here?"

"Aren't I allowed to visit my little sister?"

"Apparently not with any regularity," said Mike and instantly wished he hadn't, but not instantly enough.

"Besides," said Fay, ignoring Mike, "I do believe it's my niece's birthday."

"She has one every year funnily enough!"

"Mike?" warned Judy.

"Sorry, Fay, it's really good to see you. Honestly."

"Thanks Mike although the 'honestly' could have been omitted and who knows, I may even have believed you."

"Mike?" warned Judy.

"Fay, listen. I am so pleased to see you here with us. It's already a special day and having you here will make it even more special."

Judy kissed him. It seemed the appropriate response. Fay, caught up in the moment kissed him too. Fay stood by the car, surveying the house and when she had surveyed and presumably deliberated enough she reached inside the car for an overnight bag.

"If I may?"

"Of course you may."

Judy gave Fay a whistle stop tour of the house in which they hardly ever stopped and certainly never whistled. Fay declared herself to be impressed (very). Katy and Annabelle, bumping into Fay on the landing declared themselves impressed (very) with this sudden appearance of their aunt. Michael, who had a gift for making tea, had been busy exercising that particular gift. He had brought out a brand new set of mugs which depicted Devonshire pigs in slightly risqué poses. Feeling guilty about his rant to Susan

Jones at the museum, he had opted to buy the mugs just to show her he was quite a nice guy at heart. Looking at the mugs now, he wished he had let her think him not so nice a guy at heart.

Fay picked up her mug and brought out a pack of Richmond menthol cigarettes. "Outside?"

"Yes please," answered Judy.

Fay wandered off into the sloping garden. It was less of a wilderness than it had been six years previously, not that Fay would have known that of course. There had been a certain amount of tidying up and the shed had long since been replaced by a summer-house. The patch of concrete which formerly manfully doubled as a patio was now a fully-fledged patio in its own right. The stream still flowed at the bottom of the garden and it had been nearly six years since anyone had fallen into it. Other than that, the garden/wilderness had remained pretty much the same as per the agreement with Captain Edward de Vere Fox and his band of men...and woman.

Fay entered the kitchen looking slightly shell-shocked if indeed anyone can look slightly shell-shocked. Michael and Judy, not to mention the girls, had a reasonably good idea why she had such a look on her face.

"I've been touched...I think...by a man...I think," she announced.

The girls gave an embarrassed laugh. Judy looked embarrassed. Michael was embarrassed.

"Come on, Fay, you're forty-eight it had to happen sometime!"

79

"Very funny, Judy."

"Where were you touched?" asked Mike.

"By the stream."

"That's not what I meant, Fay."

"I know, Mike, I know," smiled Fay.

Judy gave the girls a look which said, 'what do you think, shall we tell her?' The girls gave their mum a look which said, 'I guess we have no choice.' Judy gave Michael a look which conveyed all of this. Michael didn't get it, but when Judy began speaking he did.

"Fay, you may want to sit down. You *were* touched by a man, well, almost certainly a man, but this particular man has been dead over three hundred and fifty years."

"What?" was all Fay could manage.

"We have a group of resident ghosts in our garden although they seem to see it as their garden."

"What?"

"It's true," said Annabelle, "they were buried here during the Civil War."

"What?"

"We sort of have an agreement with them," added Katy.

"What?" said Fay, whose pattern of speech was quickly becoming predictable.

"Come on," said Judy, "we'll show you if we can," as she walked towards the back door. "Coming?"

Assembling in the lower reaches of the garden, the Hamiltons together with a bewildered Fay waited. The captain, they had learned over the past six years was a perceptive fellow as befits three hundred and eighty five years of life, well, you know what I mean, and he would know exactly why there was such a gathering in 'his' garden.

"Captain!" called Michael.

"Yes," came a reply from somewhere close by. "What can I do for you, dear boy?"

"You know precisely what," said Judy. "My sister has been touched!"

"Where?"

"By the stream."

"That's not what I meant."

"I know, Captain, I know," smiled Judy. "Perhaps you can tell us which of your band of men..."

"And woman," shouted Irish Meg.

"What the...," started Fay, proving to be marginally less predictable in the garden than she had been in the kitchen.

"Sorry, Irish Meg, but I wasn't including you this time unless it was you who touched my sister which somehow I very much doubt."

"I think I can clear the matter up," said the captain, materialising close by. "It was young Thomas, you know him of course."

Everyone shook their head.

"Oh…well…we have had a lot of trouble with him over the years, the mini-skirt fiasco of the 1960's springs to mind; we nearly had a full-scale exorcism to deal with. It was eighty-seven years before he stopped chasing Irish Meg, but he has been much better of late. In his defence, he says that your sister is a most beautiful woman, in fact the most striking woman he has seen since his dalliance with Eleanor Framble before the battle of Edgehill. He couldn't help himself."

"A pretty lame excuse," observed Judy.

"Oh, I don't know though, perhaps he has a point," Fay said, with a smile.

"He has promised to behave himself in future. Silas is going to draw up a legal document which should keep him on the straight and narrow."

"Thanks, Captain. I think we can draw a veil over this episode now," Michael said, relieved that it had been sorted out so quickly.

The gallant captain faded from view with his booming, "Goodbye," lingering in the air longer than the man himself.

"Aunty Fay," said Katy, "you're just so cool. You can pull a ghost!"

"Cool? Well, I guess I am, Katy. Thank you."

"Someone in the family has to be," said Michael and instantly regretted it, but not instantly enough.

Fay understandably was full of questions and one by one they were all answered to the best of Michael and Judy's abilities and knowledge. She was suitably impressed and possibly even disappointed that neither her house in Weybridge or the bungalow in Merkuleven had resident spirits amongst their Norwegian or otherwise accessories. When Tom and Elspeth arrived, Fay was very quick to point out to her parents that she was now in on the 'secret of the garden'. Tom and Elspeth's puzzled looks did nothing to dampen Fay's enthusiasm.

"What?" said Tom and Elspeth.

Another question and answer session. More amazed and puzzled looks. Another trip to the garden. The captain was having a very busy morning of it.

"He's not been up to his tricks again already has he?"

"No, nothing like that."

"I thought not. That one's a bit old for him, I think even young Thomas would draw the line there…"

"That's my mother!" said Judy.

"Right…I…am…well…anyway, nice meeting you lovely folks, but I have to run along now." The captain duly faded away in an approximation of running.

Tom and Elspeth were assured the children were perfectly safe. That all of them quite happily co-existed with their resident

83

phantoms, although no one was quite sure how the term existence would apply to the captain and his band of men.

Whatever else the day's revelations would bring, it would also make for a lively lunch. They took a leisurely walk through Lyme and along the seafront, pausing to show Fay the sights and sounds of the town. Michael kept up a running commentary on who had done what, where and to whom. Lyme Regis has never hidden its history away awaiting discovery, it revels in it and celebrates it almost like no other town. Lyme is proud of itself.

Fay was amazed at the number of people who stopped and said hi, even if that was all they said. There were others too who seemed to know in the smallest detail what Michael and Judy had been doing.

Michael explained. "Lyme Regis has more grapevines than a vineyard."

Lunch was both leisurely and lively. Nobody could recall when they had all sat down to lunch together last. It was concluded that the difficulty in recalling the occasion was because it had never happened. Sunday lunches in East Molesey since the girls came along were Fay-free zones. Sunday lunches in Earlsfield were Fay-free zones. Sidmouth and Lyme Regis had been Fay-free zones. Fay's houses in Weybridge and Merkuleven were family-free zones. Families don't always find family life easy.

During the course of the lunch, Larissa their waitress could not help, but overhear a certain amount of birthday talk and much to Katy's embarrassment, her chocolate sponge, in addition to the deep chocolate sauce that smothered it, was adorned by a lit candle. If Katy thought her embarrassment was as deep as it could get and her face as red as it could get, she was wrong for all the diners (including a party of twelve from Chipping Norton and a group of hairy bikers from Tiverton) now burst into a surprisingly tuneful rendition of 'Happy Birthday To You'.

Katy had followed her mother to the toilet and set about gaining certain assurances from her regarding the evening's proceedings.

"You know how I love Gramps and Nanna, right?"

"Yes," agreed Judy, as she had no doubts on that score.

"And Aunty Fay, right?"

"Right, I mean yes." She had no doubts on that score either.

"They're not coming to the party are they? That would be so uncool to have old people hanging around."

"Like me and your dad?"

"No…well, yeah."

"We'll be in the restaurant downstairs in the Three Cups, but we will be keeping an eye on things as will a member of staff."

"Do you have to?"

"Yes we do!"

"Life's so unfair!"

"It is isn't it, loving family around you, more presents than you can shake a stick at and a party at a posh hotel. Very unfair, Katy."

85

"You know what I mean."

"I sometimes wonder."

The party later proved to be a success. The music was provided by Dorset Digital Discos, whose light show lit up the proceedings. The music they played was tailored to young teenagers rendering it unlistenable to anyone else, particularly Angela Treadwell who worked two evenings a week at the Three Cups to augment her pension and was spending this particular evening serving an array of soft drinks. The Osmonds,[33] now they were a proper band she reminisced, that Donny, yummy. David Cassidy too.[34] She had known that she would be in the world of showbiz herself; she would be a part of the world that she admired so much. A singer, a dancer...she had a calling to the arts. Marriage to Ian, a sheet-metal worker from Peterborough put paid to those dreams. Sheet-metal working did not quite have the glamour that she looked for. Nor did Ian.

In the middle of the floor there were thirty two girls dancing (Chelsea and Krissy had both independently decided that they didn't like Katy after all and stayed home to watch TV) with six boys watching. The six boys did not mingle. One of their number had calculated that there were 5.3333 recurring girls to each boy,

---

[33] The Osmonds are an American family music group with a long and varied career—a career that took them from singing barbershop music as children, to achieving success as teen-music idols, to producing a hit television show, and to continued success as solo and group performers.

[34] David Bruce Cassidy (born April 12, 1950) is an American actor, singer, songwriter and guitarist.

still they did not mingle. They barely spoke to each other let alone the girls, yet four of them would post variations on a theme for their Facebook statuses later: 'Wow gr8 time tonite thanx katy'. 'Party on dudes bet u wish u were there losers'. 'So tired from all that dancing and stuff. Ace.' 'that katy is lush lolz'.

As things turned out, Michael and Judy (and Fay) (and Annabelle who had not received an invitation to the party) only interrupted their meal twice to check on the proceedings upstairs. Each time they were assured by a nod of the head from Angela Treadwell that everything was as it should be and there was no sign whatsoever of illicit alcohol, something she could sniff out in seconds.

Fay had been extolling the virtues of Norwegian life not that Fay ever saw too much of Norwegian life outside of offices and factories. The virtues of Steve Newsome or otherwise were not discussed, that particular romance had now run its course, Steve proving to be nowhere near as fine as his fine dining company. Being nice to Fay's nieces ultimately counted for nothing for Steve. She now had her eyes on a Norwegian explorer recently back from the arctic. Fay, although she knew they were polar opposites and their first meeting was somewhat icy, was hopeful things would develop. It was suggested by Judy that Fay had always been unlucky in love although marginally luckier in lust. Fay agreed.

The party was over and done by 10pm. The boys had already left at 9pm. Katy thought it was great. And she almost thanked her mum and dad for making it happen. Well, to be fair, she did say thanks, but only after a little prompting.

The following morning almost everybody slept in. Judy discovered a note in the kitchen which read, 'Thanks. Love, Fay x'.

Sisters.

Earlier, upstairs, Annabelle had asked Katy how the party had been. Katy's answer was a swift kick to Annabelle's right shin.

Sisters.

Chapter Nine-Another Funeral

"I don't really see why you feel the need to go," said Judy, not for the first time as she was giving Michael one of those looks that he could not decipher.

"I feel obligated. She was an old friend of my mother's. I feel like I am representing the family," replied Michael, who didn't always find justifying himself easy.

"But you hardly knew her, you only met her once. That once when she looked after you," Judy said pointedly, for she knew only too well just how she had looked after him.

"She looked after me twice actually, but I don't suppose you want to know that do you?"

"Correct."

The funeral of Mrs (?) Sheila Barry was set for the following day. Although Michael had not thought Sheila to be particularly religious, the service was taking place at St Gabriel's in Warwick Square. He knew nothing about her family or how they had tracked him down. He had decided to take the train from Axminster. Michael didn't always find driving in London easy.

"Will you be home tonight?" asked Judy, the following morning as they were sitting in her Alfa Romeo. She was hopeful even though Michael was clutching his overnight bag.

"I'll see. Have to *gauge* how things go!"

"That's the *ticket* although knowing you, you'll run out of *steam* long before the end."

"I can see I'll have to be on my *guard* here."

"It all *points* to a victory for me."

"Don't be too sure; I can read all the *signals* you know."

"I can put you off by *siding* up to you."

"Taking advantage of my *tender*ness eh?"

"Nope, just building a *platform* for victory, Mike."

"Don't be too sure, I'm on *fireman*."

"It's no good, Mike. Winning against me is like searching for the holy *grail*. Impossible. Anyway, you'd best be making *tracks*."

Michael bowed his head in defeat, picked up his overnight bag (just in case) kissed Judy goodbye and strode towards the ticket office.

"Michael Hamilton," he announced, "there should be a ticket there for me."

"Travelling to London, sir? Ah yes, here we are. Have no time for it myself, sir."

"For what?"

"London. Have no use for it, sir."

"Oh…er…okay. Thank you."

Michael had brought a book for the journey, a biography of Henry Kissinger, but he didn't always find reading books on trains easy. He was asleep by Crewkerne. And awake at Woking. In spite of his dodgy knees he elected to walk to Pimlico from Waterloo. It was surely not that far in 1993, even allowing for those dodgy knees. St Gabriel's was full. Full of people he didn't know. Impossible to try and place them in any meaningful way, but a smattering of plain-clothes retired solicitors maybe, certainly some family. Perhaps some 'friends' who shared Sheila's proclivities and fondness for whips and other tools of the trade. He took his seat in one of the rear pews.

The service was mercifully short and feeling an intruder at the graveside he detached himself from the group of mourners and wandered around admiring the cathedral-like proportions of this fine church.

"Hello. Might you be Michael?"

He had not heard her approach. Had not even noticed her in church (separated as they were by several rows of pews). But he noticed her now. It was as if he had been transported back twenty-five years. The spiky, red hair. And the same purring voice.

"I might be. Well, not to put too fine a point on it, I am."

"Pleased to meet you, Michael. Penny, Sheila was my mother."

"I would have guessed. You are very much like her."

"In every way I am told," she purred. "We are having a few nibbles back at the house, please come and join us."

"Thank you. I may not be able to stay long though, I am hoping to get a train home tonight from Waterloo."

"Do you need a lift or are you content to walk?"

"I'll walk if it's not too far. What's the address?"

"It's mum's old house, 46..."

"...Claverton Street."

"You remember?"

"Very well," Michael said, perhaps a little too enthusiastically.

Clutching his overnight bag, he walked through the familiar streets (it's a wonder what two days all those years ago in Pimlico could do) to the aforementioned 46 Claverton Street. He made small talk with retired solicitors, he made very small talk with some of Sheila's friends who indeed shared her proclivities and were not backward in coming forward to say so. He sipped his tea and nibbled his nibbles. He listened to various reminiscences of Sheila's life, it struck him that he barely knew the woman and he once again felt an intruder.

He volunteered for washing-up duties, it being one of his skills. Penny was happy for him to take the role on; she had an aversion to Marigold gloves and washing-up.

"The colour scheme is exactly how I remember it."

92

"I have no plans to change anything. I have very similar tastes to my mother." She shot him a look which wakened memories in Michael. If only he could decipher it. She purred, he was sure of it. And she looked at him as though he was the cream and she the cat.

"We shared so many things, Michael."

"Pardon? Oh, well, that's good isn't it?"

"On occasion," she said, purring once more.

"I am sorry for your loss, Penny, especially as you were so close. Your mother was very kind to me once," Michael said, desperately trying to regain his composure.

"Yes, I know, except I thought it was twice. She told me how much she enjoyed looking after you."

"Good. I mean, did she? Good."

"Michael," she purred, becoming more feline by the minute, "If you were to stay here tonight, I could look after you."

"Pardon?"

"Oh, I think you heard me all right. How about it?"

He felt tapped like a moth drawn to flame and cream drawn to a cat. He faltered as he looked into her eyes. She put her hand on his chest. His resolve began to crumble.

"Just one night, no one will ever know. You know where the main bedroom is I believe," she added as she handed him his overnight bag.

He clutched his overnight bag and threw it down on the bed. He selected a drink from the mini-bar. The Astors Hotel in Ebury Street would do him nicely for the night. He mused on lucky escapes and his love for Judy. Especially his love for Judy.

Chapter Ten-Revelations

In which Katy may have revelled in being a teenager.

In which a rueful Annabelle may not have revelled in Katy being a teenager.

In which Michael may have revelled in some new reviews.

In which Tom may have revealed new croquet skills.

In which Elspeth may have revealed nowhere near as much as she did on 'Basque Night', as the whole of Sidmouth WI may have danced to Ravel's Bolero.

In which Fay may have discovered she has rivals for the affections of her Norwegian Polar explorer.

All those things may have happened, however, there is no Chapter Ten. Even so…

Judy, whilst ravelling her latest plot, may have received an email.

It started with an email…

Book Two

Emails.

It started with an email…

bookshop@wimbledon.org> milliganpublishinginfo@ph.com

Subject: Judy Hamilton

We are the owners of a new bookshop which is due to open very shortly in Wimbledon. We would like to have an author come along and do the grand opening for us. We thought of Judy Hamilton as her books involve Wimbledon and according to her bio she lived in the area.

Do you think that she may want to help us out?

T & D Feldman

****

milliganpublishinginfo@ph.com> judy.hamilton333@lyme.com

Subject: Bookshop opening

Hi Judy

See attached email. I don't know anything about these guys or the bookshop, but it's something you may want to do. Good publicity especially with Wimbledon coming up. Will leave it up to you. Do you want to deal with them direct?

Connor.

****

Judy.hamilton333@lyme.com> milliganpublishinginfo@ph.com

Re. Bookshop opening

Thanks Connor. I'll speak to them direct and get a date and requirements etc. If the store is set to open early I can be there and back in a day. I'll let you know if they need any books or if they are getting a supply from the wholesalers. I assume they want me to hang around and sign books and be generally pleasant!!

Judy

****

Judy.hamilton333@lyme.com> bookshop@wimbledon.org

Subject: Bookshop opening

Thanks for your invitation I received via my publisher. If I am free then I would love to come up and help you out. What date have you in mind? Is it a general bookshop or will you specialise?

Judy Hamilton

****

bookshop@wimbledon.org> judy.hamilton333@lyme.com

We hope to be open in the week commencing June 4th.....will the Wednesday of that week be okay for you? We will be selling everything.

T&D Feldman

****

Judy.hamilton333@lyme.com> bookshop@wimbledon.org

Re. Bookshop opening

June 6th works for me too. I have looked into the train times and I can be with you by 10am if that suits you?

Judy

bookshop@wimbledon.org> judy.hamilton333@lyme.com

Subject: June 6th

10am suits us very well. We will have a car and driver meet you at Wimbledon station. Thank you for agreeing to open our shop. There will be a good turnout for it we think.
T&D

****

Judy.hamilton333@lyme.com> bookshop@wimbledon.org

Re. Bookshop opening

See you on the 6th then T&D (stands for what?). Looking forward to it.

Judy

****

bookshop@wimbledon.org> judy.hamilton333@lyme.com

Re. Bookshop opening

Sorry, it's Terry and Diana. Will see you on 6th, please wait at Wimbledon station, will collect you from front entrance.

Terry and Diana

Judy.hamilton333@lyme.com> milliganpublishinginfo@ph.com

Subject: Shop opening

I have agreed to do the shop opening in Wimbledon. It's set for June8th, are you going to join me, Connor?

J

milliganpublishinginfo@ph.com> judy.hamilton333@lyme.com

Re. Shop opening.

Good god, no. Publicity is a wonderful thing, but not if it means getting my hands dirty! Hope all goes well. Have a few irons is the fire re. translations, will keep you posted.

Connor.

Departure

Michael only complained half-heartedly about the early start. Judy had elected to travel from Axminster on the six am train, even then she would be cutting it fine to be in Wimbledon by ten o' clock, but it was just possible and she could be reasonably sure that the shop would not be opening until she got there. Events such as the bookshop grand opening were to some extent unavoidable as were the various book signings that she had participated in. Some of them had involved being away overnight which she hated. Perhaps Michael, Katy and Annabelle had no real notion of how much she missed them when she was forced to be apart from them.

"You know I did another Google search last night for this bookshop of yours?"

"For crying out loud, Mike, what are you worrying about?"

"Surely if they have a well-known author opening their shop then there would be something online about it after all, shops like all businesses thrive on publicity. There is nothing, Jude. Nothing at all. It worries me."

"The website may be going live later today to coincide with the opening. They may be having technical issues. Could be a hundred and one things. I don't want to have to worry about you worrying, Mike. I'll open the shop, be impossibly charming to all and sundry, sign a few books and head back. Waterloo by four at the latest, back in Axminster by seven. Okay?"

"Okay," nodded Michael.

"I'll text you later," shouted Judy as she climbed into the carriage. "Bye, see you later, love you."

"Love you too."

In spite of her protestations to the contrary she was oddly apprehensive too about today. Yes, it was odd there was nothing tangible on the net about a new bookshop in Wimbledon. Unbeknown to Mike, she had searched through online versions of newspapers from the Wimbledon area and had drawn a blank. She couldn't even define what she felt as worry, but just a slight nagging unease. If the unease manifested itself further then there was a simple solution; get off the train at any point of the journey and return home. But she was a professional and she had entered into an agreement. She pushed her negativity away, picked up her book and sank back to read of the exploits of other people's characters in other people's worlds.

Waterloo was the usual mix of noise, organised chaos and people who seemed to be stuck like glue to the concourse. Fast food smells filled the air and lungs of everyone. Pasties, baguettes, sausage rolls, tortilla wraps, pies, burgers of every description vendors jostled for space. If she had time, Judy liked to observe. People watching is an underrated pastime, there is nothing quite like watching great surges of humanity while you are stationary with time on your hands. Time, however, was a sparse commodity for her, in fact it was fast becoming of the essence.

At Waterloo. Just dashing for train for Wimbledon. Chat later. Love you x

OK take care. Girls still in bed. See you later hopefully. X

Will let you know if there is a problem. Got my overnight stuff just in case. Must run!! Xxxx

Arrival

Late at Wimbledon, but not that late. Scanning the setting down/picking up area for a car which may be hers. There was a Ford Mondeo with a guy in it looking her way. Something didn't quite add up, but then what was she expecting? A limo? He got out and came toward her. Tall, sunglasses. No sun. Crumpled, stained jacket.

"You must be Judy," he stated.

"I am indeed. Terry?"

"No, he is waiting at the shop."

He snatched her bag and threw it in the boot. She moved towards the front, to the passenger side.

"Door sticking, best you get in the back, love."

The car stank of takeaways and stale cigarettes and goodness knows what else. She eased herself gingerly into the rear seat, barely registering the dog-ends which littered the carpet. Wrong, very wrong. By the time she registered the man sitting by her it was too late. He grabbed her wrists and pulled her towards him. A pad over her nose and mouth, a sweet smell and she was suddenly in a lift, descending wildly floor by floor. There was an alarm button she could not reach. The lift gathered speed. Time had no meaning anymore. Down below she could see darkness, the darkness came hurtling up to meet her and all sensations ceased.

When she awoke, as if from a fractured and nightmarish vision, she could not fathom where she was or what had happened to her. It felt too much like a dream still. Yet as her mind cleared, she was only too aware that this was no dream, it was a living nightmare. She was lying on a bed. Her coat, shoes and bag were gone. The bed was all the furniture the room contained. There was a window behind her, admitting hazy sunlight. Her legs refused to work at first, she half-stumbled to the window, grimly trying to co-ordinate her movements. It was like being part of a puppet show, with someone pulling her strings, jerking her up and down as they desired. She could make out the street below; it meant nothing to her. The window was locked and bolted. Hammering on it had no effect whatsoever, no one in the street below could hear her, no one was coming to rescue her. There was a door in the wall opposite the bed besides the one at the foot of it. The handle turned and she found herself in a small bathroom. There was a shower set up over the taps, a toilet which looked as though it had never been cleaned. A tremor ran through her, a hot flush enveloped her. She collapsed to her knees in front of the toilet pan and vomited until she felt empty. She lay there, not daring to move lest she bring on another attack. When she was confident there was nothing left inside her to void, she hesitantly got to her feet. With the wall for support she inched her way around the room until she regained the sanctuary of the bed. It was dark when she awoke. She swung out of the bed and tried the handle of the other door. Locked.

Terry and Dave

"Christ, that was easy, Tel."

"Yeah, so far so good. When shall we call him? Tonight?

"Or let him sweat about his precious wife for a while?"

"Mebbe, but we don't want to get him getting too rattled and calling the cops."

"There's no way in the world they could connect her to us, Tel. Besides, they would laugh at him. Wife missing, not come home, they would just think she was shacked up with some bloke for the night."

"You're right. Look, I say we call him tonight, let him know we're serious, that we mean business."

"Okay, you're on."

The brothers had history with Judy Hamilton. It was she who had reported their drug dealing outside the school. The slap on the wrist from the police did nothing to harm them, but they did suffer from a loss of reputation amongst the criminal fraternity. Even then, they had no thought of revenge, not really. In their eyes she was an interfering cow, but they adjusted, sought new patches to deal in. They were low level, mostly dealing in weed and some dubious Asian skunk, no harm to anyone really. They bought...they sold on. It wasn't as if they were into crack or roofies. They were almost like the good guys. But when they read a piece about a local author who had found a small amount of fame then they recognised an opportunity to make some cash and get even. It was perfect. The bookshop ploy was their cousin's idea. They'd have preferred not cut anyone else in on the deal, but he was family and was willing to take a lower cut. Not as if the bugger was doing much of the leg work was it, they figured. In spite of the fact that this whole operation was partly a chance to get even, they agreed to wear masks throughout. If she recognised them, it raised problems they would rather not face up to.

Terry picked up Judy's mobile from her bag. "Let's do it," he said, selecting the number under the tag, HOME. He tapped the button and listened to it ring.

Michael.

Michael's sense of unease of the morning had coloured his day. It had grown and amplified and now it was seven o' clock and the last time he had had any contact with Judy was that text from her at Waterloo station. Why had he heard nothing more? Where on earth was she? Her mobile was on permanent answer phone. Trains were running okay, he had checked that. He was not sure he could do anything else, but wait. He could do something he thought. He rang Connor Milligan.

"Hi Connor, it's Michael Hamilton. Yes, fine thank you. Do you know how the store opening went today? Oh okay. You have not heard from Judy then? Not for a while no. Yes, I am sure she will too. She didn't mention any other plans to you? Okay, no problem.

106

Have you got any contact numbers for this Terry and Diana? No? Okay, never mind. 'Night, sorry to bother you. Yes, will do."

"Heard from mum?" asked Katy.

"Not a whisper, but I'm sure she will be home soon, Katy."

"Yeah, of course. She probably forgot to take her charger, mum's hopeless like that."

"True," Michael replied, consoling himself. But there were telephone boxes; there was nothing to stop her calling.

There must have been an accident. He Googled the latest news updates covering the whole south-west area of London. Nothing that he could see that would account for Judy's 'disappearance'. By nine o' clock he was frantic with worry. His thought processes alternated between worst case scenarios and more positive outcomes. He rang her mobile again. Answerphone. He left a message. Kept it cheerful and light. The phone lit up and Judy's personalised ringtone flooded the room.

"Judy! Where are you? Are you all right?"

An unfamiliar male voice answered. "We have your wife." And Michael's world stopped turning.

"Is this some kind of j-joke?" he stammered.

"No joke. What we need from you is one hundred thousand pounds and in return you get your precious Judy back. Now, that should be nice and easy for you to work out."

"I haven't got that amount of money."

"I suggest you find it then. I'll ring in the morning at eleven o' clock and tell you how it's all going to work. And Mikey boy, don't think of calling the police not if you want your wife back in one piece."

"Can I speak to her?"

"No. Eleven o' clock tomorrow then."

The call disconnected. He picked up the phone to call the police and then thought better of it. He would do anything to ensure Judy was safe. My God, she must be so scared. How he loved that woman with every fibre of his being. She had been his life for seventeen years, he didn't feel whole without her, and in some respects he could not function without her. The girls. He had to tell them. The pain he was feeling was almost eclipsed by seeing their tear-filled eyes as they crumpled before him. He held on to them, told them how it would be all right. Their mum would be back. Tom and Elspeth. They would need to be told too. He dialled their Sidmouth number.

"Hi Tom, look I know it's late, but something has come up."

Tom listened patiently while Michael explained the situation to him.

"Make up a bed for us although I can't see any of us sleeping, we'll be over as soon as we can. I'll go and wake Elspeth and give her the news. God knows how I can do that calmly. See you soon."

Tom and Elspeth arrived within the hour. Elspeth went straight to the girls and gathered them up, enfolded them. "Come on girls, you're not to worry. We have this under control. Why don't you head to bed?"

"I've told them they can stay up, Elspeth. Like Tom said on the phone, none of us will be sleeping. I'll make some tea."

"I'll do that, Michael," offered Elspeth. "You sit down. We've got hold of Fay; she has booked a flight from Oslo for the morning."

"Now, Mike," said Tom, "the 100k, can you raise it? Because if not, I can probably come up with it. I assume you want to pay?"

"No, I do not want to bloody pay. I want Judy back unharmed. I want to beat the crap out of these guys," Michael said, fiercely. Calming, he added, "I haven't really thought about the money to be honest and if that is what it takes, then I'll pay it. Yes, I can raise it, but thank you, you two."

"If we do involve the police, there will be ways to mark the notes, dyes et cetera which means the money can be tracked."

"And if we do involve the police then all that does is place Judy in greater danger, Tom."

"Only if they find out and how the hell will they do that?"

"I have no idea, but I am not willing to take any risks whatsoever. What I say is, we wait for them to call in the morning and then we decide how to play it."

"Do we not get a say? Judy is my daughter, our daughter," sobbed Elspeth.

"Yes of course. I am just saying that we can make a decision tomorrow, the three of us."

"Five of us, dad. We're not being left out are we Annie?"

"No," said Annabelle, clinging on to her sister, who herself was comforting Elspeth.

"Five, yes of course," agreed Mike. "We wait."

Judy

Night-time. How long had she slept? She could taste the bile in her mouth. Her legs a little steadier now, she felt her way across the darkened room to the small bathroom and gulped down some water from the leaking tap. She ran her tongue over her teeth, her tongue felt twice its normal size and her mouth was dry in spite of the icy cold water she had swallowed. Fear, what else could explain it? The sound of a key being turned in a lock cut through the silence of the night. Judy retreated to the bed and curled up foetal-like against the headboard. The patch of light beyond the opening door enabled her to see two shadowy figures entering. Both were men she thought.

"Did you have sweet dreams?" mocked one of them. "Cat got your tongue, come on, we know you are awake, we heard you scampering back to the bed."

"Who are you? What the hell am I doing here? What are you going to do with me?"

"Listen, lady, we don't want to do anything with you or to you. You are a cash cow that's all. That's neat don't you think?" addressing his companion. "She's a cow *and* a cash cow."

"Very neat," the other one laughed. "All you need to know is you are here until your old man coughs up some dosh, assuming he wants you back. We have asked him for one hundred thousand for you."

"We haven't got that kind of money."

"For your sake, you had better hope he finds it...or..."

"Or what?"

"You're the writer, love, use your imagination. A sandwich for you," he said, throwing a plate onto the bed. "Hope you like cheese and pickle."

"Look," Judy said, "why not just let..."

"Don't wanna hear it love," said the taller of the two as they both left. The door slammed shut behind them. The key turned in the lock.

Judy stared at the sandwich. To eat it would seem like an act of compliance, not to eat it seemed foolhardy. The decision was made for her by her own lack of appetite. She simply could not eat. Her mind racing with every crass thought there was. What if she hadn't agreed to the book-signing? What if she had listened to the warning voice within her that morning? What if Mike could not raise the money? And her poor babies...how must they be feeling? Another fleeting thought wound its way up from her subconscious; these two men, yes the room is dark, yes they both appeared to be wearing some kind of mask, but why did she get the distinct impression she knew them?

Curled up in a ball still, she drifted into a half-sleep where reality and dreams merged and blurred. Michael, Katy and Annabelle floated across her dreamscapes, reassuringly near, but frustratingly out of reach. Their presence, if only in the remnants of dreams torn from her, was enough to give her strength for whatever lay ahead. She slept fitfully, waking often through the dark night. And now the light creeping in through the window signalled the arrival of another day. Outside, trains were rumbling into life and with them the normality of everyday life. For Judy, normality had ceased.

Terry and Dave

"Gonna ring him at eleven then, Tel?"

"Like we planned yeah unless we let him sweat a while first. It may make him more agreeable."

"Do you think he will come up with the readies?"

"I reckon he will, but I tell you something, if he says yes too quickly we'll up the price by 50k."

"Don't push him too far or he might just call the cops."

"He won't. Relax. Take her ladyship some toast or something, best make her a cup of tea."

Terry and Dave were as much in the dark as to how the day would go as any of the principals involved. The plan wasn't fool proof, they knew that, but they could hardly back out now even in spite of any misgivings they may have about the outcome. This was a big deal for them, a chance to prove themselves and make some real money instead of the piddle-arse amounts they had to make do with normally. Money so near now they could almost smell it.

Nearly eleven o' clock.

Damn signal again.

"I'll make the call outside. Dave, you wait here."

Michael

Tired, aching limbs. No one had strayed from the living-room. Everyone ached through unfamiliar sleep postures. Everyone struck dumb through worry. Hardly bearing to look at one another for fear of what they would read in each other's eyes. Fear cannot be hidden, cannot be disregarded.

"I take it your phone is one of the new generation of smart phones," asked Tom of Michael.

"Yes it is, why?"

"I was just thinking that it may be a good idea to record the call when it comes in."

"For evidence you mean?"

"Well, yes. Something like that. Have you a docking station?"

"Somewhere, yes. I'll look it out."

Elspeth filled the kettle and switched it on. Reached for a loaf and dropped some slices into the toaster. She was on auto-pilot. Bodies moved around the kitchen as in some mad, slow dance. No one mentioned Judy, no one seemed brave enough to start the ball rolling although all their thoughts revolved around her; wife, mother, daughter. They were all conscious of the ticking clock, the clock whose hands barely seemed to move. How inanimate objects mock us.

The morning seemed to last for all eternity. They were all on edge, all close to tears, close to breaking point. Eleven o' clock was still a few minutes away when the phone, now sitting in the docking station, burst into life.

"Yes," Michael shouted at it.

"Any news on our money? What's it to be?"

"I want to speak to my wife."

"No way, not possible."

"How do I know you have her? You might be a crank."

"I could pop inside and ask my mate to make her scream. I'll leave it up to him how he does it. Is that what you want me to do, Mikey boy?"

"NO!" screamed Michael, as Elspeth sobbed beside him. "Look, I can get you the money, but I need a few hours yet."

"You have all day. We'll keep our house guest a little longer. Don't worry we'll look after her Mikey boy. We'll continue our little chat this evening at five and we want the money by noon tomorrow and that's final. No bargaining. Have a good day."

"Wait...."

"Michael, can we replay the call?"

"Tom, I for one do not want to listen to some low-life threatening to harm our daughter and I do not know why you would even consider doing so."

Tom laid a hand on Elspeth's shoulder. "I feel exactly the same as you do, but I think there is something about that call that is worth listening to. So bear with me please, Elspeth."

Elspeth nodded to Michael who set about replaying the call.

"Now, listen carefully everyone," said Tom, "tell me what you hear."

"Bells," said Katy.

"Yes, church bells, but there is something else just before the chimes. Can you replay again, Michael? Thank you, now listen again."

"I hear it," said Michael. "Odd, it sounds like bells too."

"To me too," replied Tom, "except it's one bell."

"Annie," shouted Katy, "it sounds just like our old school bell, the one that one of the teachers would ring at the end of break."

"You're right, but it could be any old school," Annabelle said.

"Maybe, maybe not. Was there a church near the school? And if so, could you hear the chimes?" asked their grandfather.

"Yes there was and I'm sure we could hear chimes, but I can't really remember," replied Katy.

"Michael?"

"The school was in Tranmere Road and the church must be St Andrews. I didn't get to the school often. Judy thought highly of it which is why she almost got in a spot of bother there once. Sorry, I'm rambling."

"It's fine, Michael. What spot of bother?" asked Tom.

"She reported a pair of brothers, one of whom had a child at the school, for suspected drug-dealing. They learned who had shopped them and things got a bit unpleasant for a while. You know the sort of things; a vague threat of getting even, intimidating stares. It all fizzled out in the end and anyway, it was not long after that that we moved to Lyme. You see some relevance in this, Tom?"

"Possibly. Can we listen again please?"

"There is another sound, there just as the chimes are sounding. Traffic?" queried Michael.

"It might be a train," added Annabelle.

"I think it's two trains passing each other," said Tom with conviction.

Elspeth was becoming more and more agitated by the second and demanded to know if there was any point to all this. She really had heard more than enough of this call. To her, it was torture.

"I think we're onto something, Elspeth."

"But what? What does it mean, this talk of schools and churches? Judy could be anywhere in the country."

"She could yes, but I don't think she is, Wimbledon was a clue to that. She must be in that vicinity, it's makes sense to me anyway.

116

Michael, can you Google train times in and out of Earlsfield? See if any are due to be entering or exiting the station at eleven o' clock on a Thursday."

Michael opened up Google and a few moments later gave a cry of what sounded to them all, like triumph. "Yes, there is, but what are we saying here, Tom?"

Tom got to his feet. "What we are saying, well, what I am saying is that we are off to London. Now."

Judy

A key in the lock. One of the masked men entered. The smaller of the two.

"Breakfast," he announced as though he were some form of room service. "Slice of toast, cup of tea."

"What's happening? Have you spoken to my husband?"

"Not yet, but if he plays ball, you could be heading home. Maybe tonight if he's a good boy."

"You won't get away with it, you know."

"Keep your bloody opinions to yourself, lady. We know what we're doing. We suckered you in nicely enough didn't we? Mrs oh so bloody clever writer, you don't look so clever now do you?"

Judy offered no response to this. She offered nothing by way of eye contact. She picked up the toast and took a bite, all the time feeling his eyes boring into her. Although the situation she found herself in was totally alien to her, she knew better than to antagonise him. He

117

no doubt, would enjoy getting a rise out of her, but for Judy and her plight it would do nothing.

"You always was an interfering cow," he snarled.

"I know you," Judy blurted out before she could stop herself. "You are one of the Grant brothers. Is all this just to get your own back? Christ, it's been over six years. Why now?"

"You have money now you stupid bitch," he said, quietly, as he left the room, turning the key in the lock.

'So this was revenge', thought Judy, Another thought came to her and with the full knowledge of what she had just realised and given voice to. If they knew that she knew them, which of course they did now, then how could they hope to get away with this? There could only be one way. They could not afford to let her live. She had signed her own death warrant. Unless...

Terry and Dave

"She's recognised me, Tel, she knows who I am."

"What? You stupid twat. How? Did you take your mask off?"

"No, I swear. But she knows me, damn it, she knows me. We'll have to call it off and get the hell out of here."

"We stick with it, Dave. This time tomorrow we'll have the dosh. Nothing has changed, I won't let it change."

Even as he said it, Terry Grant knew that everything had changed. The plan may have been reasonably fool proof, but it had obviously

118

not been idiot brother proof. He could not let her go. They had to dispose of her, get the money and as Dave said, get the hell out of here. He had not bargained for this, but he was not about to give up this chance to be rich. There was no other way.

Dave, reading his brother's mind, "I'm not doing it. I don't wanna be a part of it."

"Of what?"

"You know what. Don't wanna be a part of any killing. Perhaps she won't tell."

"Yeah and pigs might fly. You don't have get your hands dirty bruv, leave it to me."

"Tell you what Tel, you go ahead and kill her if you think you have the balls to do it. And, tell you what, you keep the money. I don't want nothing to do with it, as from now."

"Clear off then, I can do this without a wimp of a brother. You just better keep your mouth shut."

"I'm no grass. I'm your brother."

"Some brother you are. Go on; piss off if you are going and good riddance."

Judy

119

If she had any hope of seeing her family again then she would have to fight back with everything she had. The younger brother, Dave she thought he was, maybe she could work on him, turn him on his brother. Terry, that was it, the other guy must be Terry. The older brother, the controlling one as she recalled. Dave may be pliable. She washed her face under cold, running water in the basin, grabbing the dirty towel which hung over the bath to pat her face dry. She opened up the cupboard under the basin, something that hadn't crossed her mind before. A toilet roll, bleach, a mouse trap and a vase. A porcelain vase, not that heavy, but something that may come in handy as a weapon if it came to it. She placed it behind the bedroom door, a plan half-forming in her head. Key in the lock, dash behind the door. One carefully delivered blow and she could be free. 'You've not beaten me yet,' she thought.

Michael,Tom,Elspeth, Katy and Annabelle.

The mood in Tom's people-carrier was fuelled by adrenalin. There was a light at the end of the tunnel. The light was fuelled by the element of surprise if Tom was right in his deductions.

"What do you think, Michael?" asked Tom, looking briefly at his son in law who was studying his tablet in the passenger seat.

"Logically, Waynflete Street looks favourite. It fronts onto the school and the church is off the southern end of the road."

"Can we narrow it down further?"

"Possibly. I think we are looking at the northern part of the road. Any further down past the church and we would have heard the traffic on Garratt Lane."

"The A217 yes?"

"Yes, Tom."

"Let's work on the assumption it's Waynflete Street then."

Elspeth was in the rear of the car with Katy and Annabelle who had absolutely refused to be left behind and in spite of misgivings on all the adults' parts they had been allowed to come. Elspeth was busy conducting a conversation on her mobile as Tom and Michael were engaged in their further deductions.

"That was Fay," she announced, "She is back in the country; she is going to join us in Earlsfield. Let me get this straight, you think Judy is being held in a house on Waynflete Street?"

"Yes we do," answered Tom.

"Because of church bells, school bells, trains and a pair or brothers, whoever they are, who may not even live in Earlsfield anymore? Do you not think we are clutching at straws here?"

"Dave and Terry Grant. That's who they are, Elspeth and guys like that tend to stick with the area they know. They'll live, work and die within a few hundred yards of where they were born. They have no horizons to broaden"

"Why don't we call the police and tell them what we know. They can pick them up or do a door to door search of the street."

"No, Nan," shouted Katy, "not if we want Mum back safely. We can't take chances can we, Dad?"

"No we can't and we won't, darling."

"I'm sorry," said Elspeth, "I don't mean to sound negative, but what is it we can do even with this so called information we have?"

Tom answered. "If we are on Waynflete Street at five o'clock when our brothers make their call, I think we can safely say we'll spot them."

"And if they make the call from inside the house? Or if they make the call from the back garden?"

"Not likely to be the back garden, Elspeth, The sound of the church and school bells would not has been as clear," replied Michael.

"They may not be on that bloody road at all!" cried Elspeth, who buried her head on Katy's shoulder, sobbing uncontrollably.

"We'll take the chance we have been given, love. Come on, chin up. If we're wrong, Michael can stall them when they call. If it comes to it, we pay up. Either way, another few hours and Judy will be here in the car with us heading back down to Dorset. Okay?"

"Okay, Tom."

They were ahead of schedule. The A303 and the M3 were reasonably quiet and with no hold ups of any consequence they found themselves crossing over the M25 at two-thirty. Although none of them professed to having any appetite, they stopped at a pub in Esher for some fortification. Fay was ahead of schedule too and rang to say she would see them in Waynflete Street long before five. Four o' clock was designated as the time to arrive and rendezvous.

Tom parked up by Townsend Mews, which backed on to the school, from where they could see a sizeable chunk of the northern part of the road near its junction with Tranmere Road. Appearing from nowhere, Fay slipped into the rear seats.

"What's the plan?"

Tom, who had taken complete charge, was sure in his own mind of what should happen when, allowing for all variables.

"We'll get out, stretch our legs and have a wander, but not as a large group. Keep your eyes peeled, look at the houses for anything unusual, but don't make it too obvious."

"Unusual how, Dad? And won't we look a tad suspicious, wandering around for a few minutes and then diving back in the car?"

"I'm not sure what I mean by unusual, Fay, maybe something that feels odd or out of place, twitching curtains, I don't know. I honestly don't think that if they are in there, they will be watching the street. They will be feeling perfectly safe. Let's do it."

In the space of a few minutes they covered the whole of Waynflete Street from Garratt Lane up to Swaby Road. Nothing had struck them as odd or out of place. Back in the car, Tom checked the time.

"Right, just before five, Michael, Katy and Annabelle will stay here. Me, Elspeth and Fay will walk up towards Tranmere Road. All we have to do is hope against hope that the call will be made outside the house."

"Why have we got to stay in the car with dad? Why can't dad and us come with you?" asked Annabelle.

123

"For one thing, we don't want your dad's phone to be heard ringing, so he has to stay here. For another, if there is trouble I'd much rather you were safe from any harm."

Ten minutes to five.

"Michael, we'll be up the road. I'll call you if we see or hear anything. And, Michael, keep him talking if you can. Good luck."

"You too. And thank you."

Five to five. Tom, Elspeth and Fay now out of sight. Michael checked his phone.

Three minutes to five. Michael, breathing hard, willing himself to keep calm, held his daughter's hands tightly.

"It's going to be all right, girls, it's going to be all right."

Five o' clock. Judy's ring tone. Michael flicked the answer button.

"Hello Mikey boy. What news for us?"

"I can get the money for you by ten in the morning, but you don't get a penny until I know my wife is safe and well. I'll need to see her before you get your hands on it."

"You seem to have forgotten that I am calling the shots here and I say what happens, when it happens and how it happens. Hold on…look can't you see I'm on the phone here, just bugger off………"

Tom, Elspeth and Fay.

Five to five.

124

"Look there," said Tom.

A man had come out of a house, two down from the junction with Tranmere Road. He punched in a number to the phone he held in his hand. Tom, Elspeth and Fay moved closer. He paid them no attention.

"Hello Mikey boy. What news for us? You seem to have forgotten that I am calling the shots here and I say what happens, when it happens and how it happens."

"Excuse me, can you help me?" asked Tom.

"Hold on...look, can't you see I'm on the phone here, just bugger off. Hey, what gives man, take your hands off me."

"Is my daughter in there? Judy, my daughter, is she in there?"

"I don't know what you are talking about, man."

"Don't bullshit me; the police are on the way, so tell me now if you know what's good for you."

"Like hell they are, old man."

"Don't be too sure about that." Tom twisted Terry's arm. "Now, is she in there?"

"Yes, yes...she's in there, top floor."

"Anyone else in there?"

"No, I swear, man. Look, here's the key, now get off me. Sweet Jesus let me go, man."

Tom released his grip and looked down at the key nestling in his hand as Terry Grant took off down the street. "We've done it, we've done it. I can't believe it. Fay, could you go and get Michael and the girls?"

"Can we please just go and get Judy, Tom?"

"No, Elspeth, that's Michael's privilege and pleasure."

"What about the police, Tom? Do we call them now?"

"We'll make a decision on that soon, when we are all together."

Michael and the girls came sprinting up the street, looks of utter delight etched on their faces. Tom thrust the key into his hand, "Top floor, all yours."

"Thank you, Tom. I don't know what to say."

"Say nothing then, just get inside and up those stairs."

"Come on girls," said Michael, "but stay behind me just in case of…well…I'm not too sure, but wait for me to go into the room and make sure everything is okay."

Judy

Judy could hear none of this, but as she heard the footsteps approaching she took up a position behind the door, vase poised. Breathing hard, she lifted the vase high above her head. Her hands were shaking so much she thought she would drop it before she had a chance to act. She took another deep breath and gripped it harder.The key turned in the lock. This is it' she thought and as the figure entered the room, she struck.

126

The tale continues.....

Chapter Eleven-Aftermath

Michael, ready to rush into the arms of Judy now suddenly found himself prostrate on the floor, dodgy knees foremost. It would be fair to say he saw stars, millions of them. In fact he imagined he was seeing distant galaxies, millions of them, in alternative universes, millions of them and they were all orbiting inside his head. Michael didn't always find being hit on the head with vases easy.

"My God, Mike, I'm so sorry, but how…what…why?"

"Why?"

"Well, maybe not why."

The door which had swung back to the closed position, now opened once more. Judy took a step away. Michael was quick to protect his head.

"Katy…Annabelle!! I don't believe it! How…what…why?"

"Why?" queried Katy.

"Well, maybe not why. How on earth did you find me? What about the guys who kidnapped me? Where are they? It was the Grant brothers you know, if you remember, Mike, I had a run in with them a few years back."

"I remember and it's your dad you have to thank really, he was the one who worked out where you were, well, maybe with a little help from me."

"Ah, Mike, my international rescue hero. I love you."

"Did they hurt you…in any way?"

"No, Mike, I am fine. If I had listened to you in the first place I wouldn't have even come up to London."

"Oh well, forget that now, I am used to not being listened to after all," he said, and regretted it instantly, but not instantly enough.

Judy, Katy and Annabelle all nodded their agreement. They did listen to Michael up to a point, even agreed with him sometimes, but invariably they did their own thing. If they had, but thought about it they would have realised that he didn't always find not being listened to easy. All the same, they all hugged him.

There was a loud knock on the door. They all sprang back. Michael's head was beginning a return to normality, the stars were still there, but mercifully stationary. The galaxies and alternative universes had retreated.

"You'll never guess who is behind the door, Jude?"

"Henry Kissinger?"

"Hah!"

"My God, Dad, Mum…but how…why?"

"Why?"

129

"Well, maybe not why."

Tom hugged Judy. Judy hugged Elspeth. Judy hugged the girls afresh. Michael hugged Judy. Katy almost hugged Annabelle. Tom hugged Michael who didn't always find being hugged by men easy. Or women come to that. Elspeth hugged Tom, a rare occurrence these days sadly.

The door swung open again. They all sprang back.

"If only there was a tree in the middle of the floor you could all hug that."

Fay!" exclaimed Judy. "I've heard of unexpected family gatherings, but this is just getting silly."

Judy hugged Fay, but there the hugging ended for now.

"I found your coat and bag downstairs, Judy," said Fay, handing over the items in question in a business like fashion as befits the acting CEO of Stammersson Inc. "Shall we go? I have a plane to catch."

"Back to your arctic explorer, Fay?"

"Maybe, but I'm beginning to think we are poles apart, Judy. The whole thing could be a (frozen) waste of time."

Elspeth brought up the subject of the brothers Grant and the problem of whether to place the whole affair in the hands of the police. Elspeth was very much in favour, it's what any self-respecting member of the WI would do. Everyone said so. Tom thought that no good would come of it, in his opinion they were very unlikely to go down this road again (kidnapping, not

Waynflete Street). Michael, although he would like to see justice done, was in general agreement with Tom. Judy herself was all for letting sleeping Grants lie.

Terry Grant, in fact, spent the next few weeks in virtual hibernation, scared of his own shadow. Gradually, he returned to his life of petty crime and his low-level dealing. It was unfortunate that he owed so much money. It was doubly unfortunate that he owed much of it to 'Big Sam' who ruled Merton, Earlsfield and Wimbledon with an iron fist, not to mention wooden baseball bats. When the debt had risen too much and too quickly he despatched a couple of his 'colleagues' whose persuasive abilities were second to none. Everyone said so on the local casualty ward.

When they knocked on Terry's front door, he ran out the back door, not even pausing to open it. (They don't make back doors like they used to.) For all anyone knows, he is still running although there have been rumours through the years particularly with reference to the new flyover on Staines bypass.

Dave Grant, on the other hand, turned over a new leaf. He certainly would have surprised Michael by the mere fact of his moving away. He was a bit, but only a bit, of a car mechanic and when his cousin Craig, who owned a garage in Filey, said he was looking for staff, Dave jumped at the chance. Not that he knew where Filey[35] was, but he was in good company there, not many people know where it is. He prospered; he married, had children

---

[35] Filey is a traditional English seaside resort with a friendly atmosphere, offering restful 'get away from it all' holidays. A fishing town on the North East coast of England, Filey has enjoyed a reputation of being a seaside resort since Victorian days.

and never mentioned his brother again although his wife caught him smiling once when they negotiated the Staines bypass on one of their trips down south to see what remained of his family.

With the most perfunctory, yet heartfelt, of goodbyes Fay departed for her Norwegian furniture and accessory-free house in Weybridge and from there to Heathrow, arriving in Oslo in the early hours. After snatching a few hours' sleep, she would be on her way to Fredrikstad. Somewhere over the North Sea her seating companion, Derek Bradbeer a businessman from Basildon who specialised in models of famous Vikings in history, who had spent the majority of the flight attempting to chat her up with tales of Eric the Red and Hasslom the Horned One would hear her sigh and say 'Judy' with an audible grin.

Tom's people carrier sped through the evening, although with Elspeth at the helm there was precious little speeding going on. As they pushed on past Guildford, the consensus of opinion was that they were all starving. They stopped at a pub alongside the Hog's Back[36] for a hog roast, as much as they could eat. They went the whole hog in fact with Judy quite naturally hogging the limelight.

Katy and Annabelle were of the opinion that having a mother kidnapped was just about as cool as it could get. Michael was of the opinion that having a wife kidnapped was about as stressful and terrifying as it could get. Tom and Elspeth agreed. Judy was of the opinion that she would rather just forget the whole thing, thank you very much. The girls were duly warned not to breathe a

---

[36] The Hog's Back is a part of the North Downs in Surrey that lies between Farnham in the west and Guildford in the east.

word...ever. They were both of the opinion, but especially Katy, that life's so unfair.

"What about Connor, Jude are you going to tell him what happened?"

"No way, Mike. He would have a press release prepared in seconds and email it to everyone from *The Times* to the *Morning Star*."

Michael was busy imagining the *Daily Express* relegating the headline HEATWAVE EXPECTED...THOUSANDS MAY DIE to page five and running with MODERATELY WELL KNOWN AUTHOR KIDNAPPED. Yes, best not tell Connor.

Tom elected to drive when they resumed their journey. By the time the twinkling lights of Lyme Regis shone beneath them all of the occupants of the car were fast asleep with the exception of Tom which was fortunate indeed.

Chapter Twelve-A Revue Review

"I'm quite excited about tonight," said Michael. "About this revue review I mean."

"I knew what you meant, Mike. I remember the time when you said that being excited was something to do with me!"

"Hah! It still is."

"You forgot to add the word occasionally. About tonight though, come on now, it's just a review, you have done hundreds."

"I know, but this is like a trial run for getting back into it full-time. I want to do myself justice. It's important."

"It's a revue by the Lyme Regis Strolling Players not the State Opening of Parliament."

"I'm still excited, Jude."

"No need to make a *song and dance* of it, not with the *sketch*y information on the content you have."

"Very good. I know it's a throwback to the old days of revue."

"There should be quite a *variety* on show then."

134

"Jude, you've let yourself down there on the wordplay front, variety and revues are two very different things. Well, not that different admittedly. A revue usually has a theme running through it. This one, rather predictably, has a seaside theme."

"I'm *shore* you will love it."

"Hah! Not convinced I can rise to this wordplay, I have a lot on my *brine*."

"Oh *buoy* that was bad even for you!"

"And there's me thinking it was going *swimming*ly and I was *current*ly in the lead."

"Thinking of yourself again, Mike I see, you are so *shell fish*. You should *sea kelp* for that you know."

"I'm not rising to the *bait*, Jude. You are only *fishing* for compliments."

"It ap*piers* you have no idea. You are *flounder*ing."

"Don't give me that old *line*. I just think when it comes to wordplays that I have been *delta* bad hand."

"Very good. You poor *sole*, but at least you have the *quay* to my heart."

"You win, as always."

"Thank you, Mike my wordplaying hero."

"Have you decided whether to come tonight yet?"

"I checked my diary, Mike and what do you know? I have found I have a prior engagement."

"Which is?"

"I'm washing my hair."

"Odd that, every time there is a musical on at the Marine Theatre you are washing your hair then, too."

"You know me and musicals. All the characters know the words to all the songs, how could they? They dance around in the middle of the street without a care, why would they? They know all the steps, how could they? And worst of all…"

"Yes?"

"They all get married in the end, why would they even want to? And then they feel compelled to sing about it!"

"Yep, about as realistic as a spy who is also a Grand Slam winning tennis player," said Michael and instantly wished he hadn't, but not instantly enough.

"I'm off to my study to further my career in unrealistic writing," said Judy dismissively and turned on her heel and went. Not that she had heels on, not in the house or anywhere else for that matter. Although turning on one's slippers does not quite work somehow when leaving both a husband and room dismissively.

Michael ruminated once more on this increasing ability of his to say hugely inappropriate things. Were there pills for this? Or should he just engage his brain before opening his mouth? He had no doubts which of these options his family would go for. He left

Judy to her own (plot) devices and took himself off to the seafront. A brisk walk and a brisk pint would do the job nicely. The walk turned out not to be so brisk, not with his dodgy knees and the three pints of cider in the Royal Standard rivalled the walk for its not so briskness. He was fully aware that Judy may not be best pleased with him cider drinking without her, the simple solution was not to tell her. He bought three packets of ultra strong burn your mouth mints which were guaranteed to not only freshen your mouth, but disguise every trace of food and drink known to man.

"Hey Jude. All right?" was his scintillating greeting as he encountered Judy in the kitchen.

Judy sniffed. "Nice cider, Mike? Or was it two?"

"Three actually. Sorry about earlier, of course there is realism in your novels."

"Look, Mike, I know full well my writing is not exactly fully grounded in realism, but I try to make each individual part work in its own world. What bothers me is that your remarks are based on jealousy and I don't like it, Mike, I don't like it at all. Would you rather I gave it all up?"

"No of course not. Sorry, I just find myself saying the wrong things at the wrong times. Do you think there are pills for that?" he asked with a smile.

"No, just engage your brain before you open your mouth, you silly man."

He kissed her, it seemed the appropriate response.

Katy and Annabelle sauntered in, separately of course. If they were not actually involved in an argument, then they were very often on the verge of an argument, which could be about the most trivial of things. Although not trivial to them by any means. Today's dispute revolved around the merits of Zak Curry, a newcomer to Katy's school and also a neighbour. In Katy's eyes he was a Greek god minus the long white beards they were wont to have. In Annabelle's eyes, he was a dork of the highest order.

"He is not a dork, he's cute."

"You're a dork yourself Katy, that's why you like him. And have you seen his spots? Ewwww…"

"You're just jealous cos no boy in his right mind would look at you twice."

"Yeah, well, I'm not interested in boys anyway so there."

"Just as well then as they are not interested in you."

"Girls, do we have to go through this ritualistic arguing day in and day out?"

"She started it," said Annabelle.

Katy had a somewhat contrary view.

"I don't care who started it, but you can both finish it. Right?"

Katy and Annabelle remained obstinately dumb.

"Are you giving your poor dad a hard time, girls?" asked Judy as she re-entered the room. "That's enough, right?"

"Right, mum," they said, rather sheepishly.

"How do you do that, Jude?"

"Watch and learn, Mike, watch and learn."

He wished he could. Well, he could watch of course, but as for learning, he doubted it.

After dinner (chicken breasts and roast vegetables) Katy and Annabelle retired to their rooms, glad to be free of each other's company. Judy retired to her study for some demented scribbling (she had lied about washing her hair). Michael strolled down to the Marine Theatre for the Lyme Regis Strolling Players' Seaside Revue.

There was a noticeable buzz of anticipation from the audience who were busy selecting their seats with care. There was a lack of buzz of anticipation from Michael who was busy selecting his bar stool with care. The proximity of the bar counter to the bar stool he selected was not uppermost in his mind, but rather it was the vantage point said bar stool gave him for an overview of the stage. Michael didn't always find convincing himself easy, but he did try, he really did.

He expected hoary old jokes, hoary old songs and hoary old dance routines. He was not disappointed. His low expectations were admirably met. The evening was awash with fluffed lines, fluffed dance steps and fluffed stage directions. If there was a stage manager present, something Michael had the gravest doubts over, he or she must have been tearing out his or her hair on various occasions.

He did, however, have a nagging thought and it was this; could he ever envisage getting up on stage and performing in front of his peers as these people had? The cast was full of disparate folk; a solicitor, a builder, a teacher, six shop assistants, one Post Office clerk, two chefs, a barmaid, an architect, a former antique shop owner from Chipping Norton although she was not that antique. So what if they fluffed the occasional line? They gave it their all from the opening strains of 'Oh I do like to be beside the seaside' to the closing all-singing, all-dancing finale of 'Sur la Plage'. He had to be kind to them surely. Would Johnny Norfolk have kicked the ball out of play because the rival goalkeeper was injured in the penalty area? Would Johnny Stevens have let the KGB agent, Viktor Poliakov go because he had a wife and three children waiting for him at home in Omsk? He thought they might. They had not resided in Michael's head for thirty five years without picking up something of his character.

His revue review when it appeared was couched in such terms so that most people reading it would believe he had enjoyed the revue very much indeed. Words such as enthusiasm, zeal, eagerness, energy and earnestness liberally sprinkled throughout the review enabled Michael to be true to his reviewing self. Johnny Norfolk and Johnny Stevens would have been proud of him. Even Judy would have been. And she was.

Chapter Thirteen-Chapter and Verse or Worse

"Let me get this right, you haven't brought a change of clothes. Is that what you are saying?" asked the officious young man with the officious looking clipboard.

It was indeed what Judy was saying. He was right in that respect.

"But it would have been in the emails, sweetie. It was just below the approved limits for the mini-bar in your dressing room. You must have seen it."

Judy had not seen it. He was wrong in that respect.

"The emails went through my publisher, Connor Milligan. He didn't mention a change of clothes," Judy offered, realising how lame this sounded.

The officious young man with the officious looking clipboard thought this excuse very lame. Judy was right in that respect.

"But you do know you are appearing in two shows, yes?"

Judy did know that and she wasted no time in telling him so.

"So, tell me when you think your second appearance will be?"

"Something tells me it will be today."

"Correct. I'll wander down to the wardrobe department, well I say department, but it has more in common with a cupboard mostly because it is a cupboard. There may be something there we can utilise."

This was Judy's introduction to the television quiz show *Chapter and Verse or Worse*, a light-hearted, some would say humourous look at the world of literature. Less unkind souls would label it humourless. A young woman approached Judy.

"I'm Alice," she announced, offering Judy a firm handshake. "Programme assistant. I'll tell you what's happening when and introduce you to how it all works. We'll get you to make up first."

"Make up what?"

"No, I mean take you to have your face and hair made up...oh, you were being funny weren't you."

"I was trying. To be honest, I'm not a make-up kind of gal. I prefer the natural look."

"The natural look is one thing, but trust me love, you need a little extra something for the cameras to love you. And believe me they have to love you. I suppose they might just in your case."

Judy was not sure whether she had been insulted or complimented so decided on silence and a certain amount of compliance. She was led off to make-up, like a lamb to blusher. There, the officious young man with the officious looking clipboard caught up with her.

"I've not had much luck," he said, "all I can offer is a Dorothy costume from a 'A Wizard of Oz' production and a banana outfit."

142

"I quite like the look of gingham dresses on me, but I'm not too sure about wearing those ruby red slippers. They're so not me."

"It's no problem. Neither the studio audience or the viewers will see them. Oh…you were being funny weren't you."

She was. He was right in that respect. "Trying, yes. I'll just wear this outfit of mine for both recordings. There can't be any harm in that surely."

The officious young man with the officious looking clipboard looked Judy's outfit up and down and was of the unspoken opinion that there may well be lots of harm in it. With a scarcely concealed sniff of disapproval he walked away.

Alice collected Judy after the studio's make-up artist had struggled valiantly with her and had admitted defeat. "You don't look any different," Alice said, also with a sniff of vague disapproval. "Right, now you should meet your fellow guests."

Judy was led to a small lounge which had all the appearance of a doctor's waiting room. There was even a six months old copy of *Good Housekeeping* and three even older *National Geographics*.

"Clara, this is Judy Hamilton. I'm sure you have heard of her."

Clara Snelling also wrote novels in the espionage genre, in her case with a twist in the tale or to be more accurate, the tail. Her spy thrillers had liberal helpings of all manner of fetishes and regular bouts of BDSM, something Bradley Steel would never approve of, but possibly something Mrs (?) Sheila Barry would have enthused over. Her latest, *Thirty Days in Mandalay* was being lapped up by an adoring public. The newspapers all acclaimed her hero, Daniel

Ryan, as being a James Bondage for the modern age. Shaken, stirred and whipped.

"Ah yes, Judy Hamilton," she said, as though the name was in some way distasteful to her. "You write...those...er...um..."

"Books?" offered Judy.

"Don't tell me...it's coming to me...thrillers in the tennis world." She too sniffed with mild disapproval.

'Perhaps everyone is coming down with a cold,' thought Judy idly.

The other member of the panel was Raymond Stevens (no relation) who wrote what the press called 'serious' novels about 'serious' issues. Raymond Stevens seemed just a little too high-brow for this decidedly low-brow show. His publisher however had urged Raymond to consider doing the show to help spearhead a campaign to make the general public more generally aware of his books. Raymond therefore was performing under sufferance which had the effect of making him even more insufferable than he had been previously. Still, on the plus side, he had heard of Judy too. But, just as with Clara Snelling he had not deigned to read any of her work.

The question master was Jeffrey Hopper, a failed stand-up comedian, a failed chat show presenter, but a tolerable quiz master. The assistant producer went through the format with the panellists. Keep it lights folks, this is not *The Book Review*, be topical, be funny, but not too funny. Jeffrey has to get 71% of the laughs, it's in his contract.

144

The floor manager set up the camera angles, checked the panellists postures, noted Judy's lack of make-up and sniffed disapprovingly. Judy was as nervous as she had ever been, not even fully understanding what was required of her, for unlike her fellow guests she had never seen the show. The producers had sent a DVD of the previous series, but these Connor had not forwarded. Still, she was a natural, everyone said so in the studio. And reassuringly, there was an editor attuned to the faintest blip or error who could carpet the cutting-room floor with embarrassing or otherwise unworthy footage. It was his job too to ensure the loudest laughter coincided with Jeffrey Hopper saying something he perceived to be funny. Judy was in safe hands. The seconds counted down...

The warm-up man, a failed quiz master and failed chat show host, but a tolerable stand-up comic had kept the studio audience on the edge of their seats, wondering when the quiz would start. It was now.

Jeffrey Hopper greeted the small studio audience and much larger (although not that much larger) television audience with an affability honed during the previous eighty-four editions of the show. There were ripples of applause for Clara Snelling and Raymond Stevens. Then it was Judy's turn. A light flashed on top of the camera which seemed to be intent on examining her nasal hair in minute detail. She smiled as Jeffrey introduced her as an upcoming star of the literature world, one whose following was bound to grow. She nodded, not in agreement, but just for the chance to give her head something to do. She smiled, hoping Jeffrey had reached the end of his embarrassing eulogy.

"First round then, folks. I give you each a random phrase and you have twenty seconds to use it within a well known quote from

145

any piece of literature you like. We'll start with you, Judy. Your phrase is 'a bear hug'."

She couldn't remember the last time her mind had been so blank. Or if it had ever been so blank. She was well read. Everyone said so. There must be a quote she knew and loved that she could adapt. She smiled as the camera captured every nuance of the dilemma that her face displayed.

"Ah, yes," she started confidently, "A bear hug won't be a bear hug without presents, grumbled Jo."

The studio audience sniggered.

"Thank you, Judy," oiled Jeffrey Hopper, "a good effort although a tad lacking in humour."

"They laughed," she said, pointing at the audience.

"They'd laugh at anything," Jeffrey replied.

To prove his point, the studio audience went into hysterics. If the aisles had been wide enough they would have been rolling in them.

"I see what you mean, Jeffrey," said Judy, warming to her task.

The studio audience laughed uncontrollably at this. Judy was worried in case some of them became physically ill as a result. There has no doubt been a study of how being exposed to high levels of mirth can result in major and long-lasting damage to the body's immune systems.

Judy fared a little better in the following round, 'Famous writers in uncharacteristic poses', although deducing it was F. Scott

146

Fitzgerald in the gorilla suit was more of an inspired guess rather than due to any well-informed reasoning. Add to that, a successful bout of miming in the final round (*East of* Eden, no easy thing to mime the closing paragraphs of) and not even Jeffrey's opening line in the second show of "nice outfit, Judy...is it new?" (which predictably was followed by gales of laughter from the studio audience) could dampen Judy's enthusiasm for the whole television experience. She thought that she could even be persuaded to take part again when invited. Alas, the invitation never materialised.

Chapter Fourteen-Present Day

A sunny summer's morning. Michael and Judy had been up a while and were sipping tea on the patio. All was quiet and peaceful apart from a whispered hello from Irish Meg, who they often heard, but had never, ever seen.

"It's odd you know," said Judy.

"I'm sure it is, but give me a clue."

"I have just finished talking to Fay on the phone."

"Fay Weldon?"

"Hah! Very funny. Do you know what she told me?"

Michael didn't always find guessing easy and today was no exception.

"She read in the local press that Eddie Fox had died. And do you know what?"

"No, but I have a feeling you are going to tell me." He was quick like that.

"Last night I heard singing outside."

"Let me guess," offered Michael, suddenly finding guessing easy. "You think you heard the captain duetting with Eddie Fox in our garden?"

"With a backing singer or singers!"

"Henry Kissinger and the Vandellas? Fay Weldon and the Pips?"

"Hah! No, Irish Meg for one!"

"No Derek 'Buddy' Valentine on drums?"

"Not that I was aware of, but then I could have been dreaming anyway. It's just that some of the singing was off-key so I thought of Eddie Fox naturally."

"Naturally. Let's hope it was just a dream, I'm not sure I can put up with Eddie Fox serenading us forever more. Is Fay honouring us with a visit?"

"Meaning?"

"Er...meaning it would be an honour to have her here of course."

"You really need to beep when you reverse like that you know. No, she is flying back out to Norway in two days, it was a quick visit to Stammersson's mainstore. She just rang to see how I was after...well...you know."

"And how are you? It's been a while, but you don't talk about it."

"I am fine, Mike, really. If I want to talk about, you'll be the first one I come to my international rescue hero. I am glad that I have been able to write again now though. Sure you are all right with that?"

"I am perfectly fine with it."

"Not jealous?"

"Insanely, but I'll get over it!"

"Good boy. Now, guess what day it is," Judy said, and gave Michael a look which was meant to convey to him exactly what this day was and what it meant. It didn't work.

"It's Saturday," answered Michael correctly. His day recognition could never be faulted. Everyone said so.

"It's six years today that we moved to Lyme Regis!"

"Really?"

"No, I said that just to waste your time. Yes, of course, really!"

"Should we celebrate?"

"Yes, you go and wake the girls while I put my thinking cap on."

"Tell you what, you go and wake them. I think you will be more successful."

Michael didn't always find waking his daughters easy, particularly early on a Saturday morning. Well, it was actually eleven o' clock, but for Katy and Annabelle being called at this hour this would seem unfeasibly mean. Annabelle would be grumpy for a while and Katy would be grumpier for considerably longer with the occasional 'life's so unfair' thrown in for good measure.

Judy, normally so efficient at waking her daughters, certainly in comparison with Michael, had to admit defeat on this occasion for there were no daughters to wake up. The beds were unmade and incredibly messy so she could be tolerably sure they had been slept in, but as to where they were, now that was puzzling. They were not known normally for doing things quietly, but she supposed they could have slipped out of the house while Michael and herself had been trying to do things quietly earlier.

Michael was now in the kitchen running through the options for the day, he had never found decision making easy.

"The girls aren't there, Mike."

"What...you don't think?"

"No of course not."

"But you don't know what I'm thinking."

"Oh, Mike, I always know precisely what you are thinking and in this case you are wrong."

Judy's phone beeped.

are u guys out of bed yet.

"It's Katy," said Judy.

Yes and it's you not u and where is your question mark? And where are you? Is Annie with you? X

151

were waitin for u x

It's we're not were and you not u (again) and where are you?

at the new seafood place in gardens jst cum down

No capital letters on your phone, Katy? And it's just not jst and come not cum.

All of which Judy relayed to Michael who was as puzzled as she was. They both were perplexed as to what their daughters may be up to, but they wisely came to the decision there was only one way to find out.

Within a few minutes they declared themselves ready without any firm idea of what they were ready for. The 'Prawn Cracker' restaurant fortunately served up imaginative dishes as opposed to its rather less than imaginative name. It had proved a hit locally and the clientele was growing both in numbers and stature after food critics in the national press discovered its delights. Inevitably there had to be a rise in prices. The people who read the glowing reviews in the *Observer* or the *Sunday Times* fully expected to pay through the nose for such culinary delights in such a fine setting. The owner of the restaurant, Oliver Valvona, a chef who had recently been running his own establishment in San Sebastian specialising naturally in the cuisine of the Basque country, saw no good reason to disappoint them in their desire to pay top money for top food.

Judy's phone beeped.

wen u gettin here x

Judy tapped out a reply.

Soon and it's when not wen, getting not gettin and try to remember your question marks. X

yeah rite whatever x

AAAAARRRRRGGGHHHHHHHHHHH!!!!!!!!!! Xx

When they entered the 'Prawn Cracker' Michael and Judy were met with the somewhat incongruous sight of Katy and Annabelle wearing a hybrid combination of school uniform and high fashion. Katy took their coats (it's summer in Dorset...you have to be prepared) and Annabelle showed to them a table by the window which gave the best and most extensive views available to the 'Prawn Cracker's' diners.

"What on earth is going on, Annie?" asked Michael.

"Me and Katy thought that with all that has gone on this year, you know," she said, lowering her voice, "with mum and all that kidnap stuff, that we would treat you to a nice lunch."

"And," added Katy, as she arrived at the table, "it's six years today that we moved here so Happy Anniversary to all of us."

"Thank you so much, girls, but how can you possibly afford it?"

"We have both been saving a bit from what dad gives us."

"I can see I'll have to reduce your allowance," said Michael good-humouredly. "I still can't see you affording a lunch here for four though."

"Well, we had a little help and it's not lunch for four, it's six."

On cue a waiter appeared busying himself laying the table. On cue Tom and Elspeth Kennedy appeared.

"Dad, Mum! Wow, this is turning into some day isn't it Mike?"

Michael agreed. He was good like that. He knew a good day when he saw it.

"Katy and Annie rang me and asked what I thought and I thought it was a marvellous idea. I made the reservations and here we are," said Tom.

Judy beamed at her girls. Tom beamed at Judy. Michael beamed at Elspeth. Katy even beamed at Annabelle. The waiter beamed at everyone, that's what they do.

"Excuse me, you have laid out seven places, it's actually lunch for six," Michael said, completely in the dark about the look the waiter was giving him.

"Actually, Mike, it's lunch for seven."

"Bloody hell, Fay!"

"Hello folks and Happy Lyme Regis Anniversary."

Judy stood up and pressed her head to the glass. She took in the view, the almost impossible beauty of the place. She turned around and took in the view of her almost impossibly wonderful family. She is almost certain she said thank you to each and every one of them in turn although no sound appeared to have left her mouth.

"Oh Katy, Annie, thank you so much, you are incredible daughters and incredible people, I love you dearly."

"Thanks, mum, we love you too, don't we Annie?"

"Well of course we do!"

"Tell me, girls," said Michael, "does this mean you are going to get along better now? Have all hostilities ceased?"

"Back to normal tomorrow, dad. sorry," answered Katy, "right, Annie?"

"Right, Katy, but give me a chance to buy some shinguards first please."

They both laughed. Michael and Judy laughed. Tom and Elspeth laughed. Even Fay laughed. The waiter smiled.

The waiter, still beaming as they do, poured champagne into five glasses. Katy felt very hard done by, but decided she would not say 'life's so unfair. Not today. That really would be unfair.

"Who's going to propose a toast then?" asked Elspeth.

Michael rose to his feet. This was the kind of moment that Johnny Norfolk and Johnny Stevens revelled in. Various Footballer of the Year and Spy of the Year ceremonies had benefited from their witty and heartfelt speeches.

"I could happily drink a toast to every one of you, several times over. You all in your own ways make my world a brighter, happier place. I have to echo what Judy said and say that Katy and Annabelle enrich our lives so much. You all do. Now, I must ask you to raise your glasses...oh yes...girls, you'll have to use water…yes I know, Katy, life's so unfair…and toast my beautiful woman, Judy. To Judy!"

Judy turned away once more.

"Judy, are you crying?" asked Michael, perceptive as ever.

"Of course I'm bloody well crying. Life's too good not to cry isn't it? Well, isn't it?"

He kissed her. It was as ever, the appropriate response.

Chapter Fifteen-Timeline:

1973: Michael Arkle Hamilton born.

1975: Judith Anne Kennedy born.

1984: Michael creates his alter-egos: Johnny Norfolk and Johnny Stevens.

1987: Judy begins to take an interest in boy bands.

1989: Michael begins to take an interest in Sarah Higginson and vice versa resulting in the summer of frolicking.

1990: Michael begins work for the *Cheltenham Post*

1991: Judy begins to take an interest in boys.

1992: Michael finds new employment with *Oxon Folk.*

1992: Judy learns Klingon from Christopher Drummond and learns much more besides from Jason Wilkins.

1993: Michael encounters Mrs (?) Sheila Barry and begins a new job as chief reviewer for '*The Big Brash Guide To London*' He purchases his Canford Road flat in Clapham.

1993: Judy delves into the world of insurance and encounters Mrs Danvers. She then enters the world of education and encounters Miss Roseberry, Mrs Danvers's evil twin.

1993-2003 Not much happens. Michael remains at '*The Big Brash Guide To London*' and Judy remains at *St Botolph's School, Chessington* where she spends some of her time sticking pins into a wax effigy of Miss Amanda Roseberry.

1995: Something did happen after all. Judy joined the Sealed Knot.[37]

2000: Judy moves into her Manchuria Road flat in Clapham.

2003: Spring: Michael and Judy meet at Clapham Junction station.

2003: Autumn: Michael proposes. Has to replace coffee table. Judy accepts.

2004: Spring: Michael and Judy marry. They honeymoon in Venice.

2005: Tom Kennedy is under suspicion in the city and viewed with suspicion in East Molesey.

2006: Katy Louise Hamilton is born.

2007: The family move to Earlsfield. Michael becomes editor of '*The Big Brash Guide To London*'. Judy leaves *St Botolph's* for good.

2008: Annabelle Emma Hamilton is born.

2013: Margaret Hamilton dies after a short illness. The family pay a visit to Lyme Regis. They move to Lyme Regis. Judy goes back to work as a teaching assistant. They meet their 'garden guests.' Fay

---

[37] I'll explain later.

begins work for Stammersson Inc. and divides her time between Weybridge and Frederikstad.

2015: Judy writes her first novel.

2016: Judy writes her second novel and begins to scale down her teaching assistant duties

2017: Michael takes tentative steps back into the world of reviewing. Judy completes her third novel and gives up work. Not that writing isn't work of course. Michael joins the staff of *Devon World*. Tom and Elspeth host their retirement party and duly retire to Sidmouth. The infamous 'Basque Night' takes place.

2018: Geoffrey Hamilton dies in the spring. Michael attends the funeral of Mrs(?) Sheila Barry in Pimlico.

2019: Katy, with a surge of optimism becomes a teenager. Annabelle suffers a multitude of bruised shins. Judy is kidnapped. Judy is rescued by her family.

2019 onwards: See next chapter.

Chapter Sixteen–Future Days

What of the future I hear you ask? Michael and Judy remained there in the old house. For them it was the perfect family home, even when it was no longer strictly speaking a family home save for the occasional visits by daughters, grandsons and granddaughters. Oh yes, I was coming to that.

Katy and Annabelle survived their teenage years when life was so unfair for them as testified to by the endless arguments, silences and bruised shins (Annabelle's). Katy persevered through school battling both dyslexia and inherited dodgy knees to go on to university and there she obtained a degree in performing arts. She never became a big star admittedly, the invitations to various reality TV shows never materialised, and her cardinal sin as far as that type of show was concerned, was that of never being a real celebrity anyway. Not that she cared about that.

She had her children; Jason (his grandmother shuddered every time she heard the name), Chloe and a husband, Jake who she met when they were both in a touring production of '*Ophelia Get Your Gun*'[38] a not wholly successful mix of Shakespeare and the Wild West. Home was in north Cornwall, a converted barn which wore

---

[38] Two excerpts coming up soon, you may judge for yourselves.

its agricultural past on its sleeve or more literally on its drive where a bright yellow combine harvester greeted visitors along with various implements whose usage was to remain unknown. Visitors were encouraged to give their best shots at guessing how these implements would have been used and a box was provided in the kitchen where such guesses could be dropped. The practice was discontinued when the content of some of these estimates was found to be a tad unsavoury.

Annabelle, who not blighted by either dyslexia or dodgy knees, proved academically the stronger sister. Shades of her mother and Aunty Fay. There were months if not years of indecision in her teens. Should she become a vet or a doctor? A nurse? A physiotherapist? The choices narrowed; a vet or a doctor? Tricky. Annabelle herself was probably the most surprised out of anybody when she joined the police force; walking the beat though was not for her. Her degrees enabled her to go straight into 'middle-management' (an Inspector to you and me). She would rise through the ranks to become one of the youngest ever superintendents since, well, forever. Along the way she too collected children, Rosie and Daniel plus a husband, Stefan. If you need proof that theatre brings people together, look no further for Annabelle met Stefan (as she ran for the toilet; very much her mother's daughter) as she watched Katy in '*Ophelia Get Your Gun*'[39]. Stefan, in fact had already seen it three times proving that theatres can attract the strangest of people.

Geoffrey Hamilton's poems were to find a wider audience when Connor Milligan was persuaded by Judy to publish them in a handsome volume edited by Michael, it was one of Michael's

---

[39] Two excerpts still coming up very soon, p166 in fact.

proudest moments. The collection was reckoned to be one of the finest volumes of poetry by a posthumous Cotswolds author. Everyone said so.

Tom and Elspeth Kennedy retired to Sidmouth as we know. Elspeth set about instilling some vigour into the local branch of the Women's Institute, threatened momentarily during the Basque Night debacle. Although she bounced back from that night of embarrassment with her usual fortitude and lemon drizzle cakes of wonder. Whilst Tom was to become something big in the bowling club and something less big in the croquet club. They were regular visitors to Lyme Regis, they had both warmed to Michael over the years and they were extraordinary grandparents, devoted to Katy and Annabelle in a way that surprised everybody. Elspeth died after a series of strokes and Tom lingered on in the Coburg Terrace home for a few years, fiercely independent. He did however have a woman who came in 'and did for him' although history is silent on what she 'did for him'.

Fay went on to be the CEO of Stammersson Inc and made a huge success of it, but there was to be no marriage (although a few lovers and not just restricted to the worlds of catering or polar exploring) or children. For all her achievements that her parents were immeasurably proud of, she felt she had somehow disappointed them, no longer the golden girl. Eventually she settled in Norway and a few years later retired to Harstad. From there she set off one morning for a day's walking around Vågsfjorden. She never returned.

Judy continued to write her tennis-cum-spy thrillers although the output dropped in later years. She never quite got around to believing her good fortune. There were to be a few more television appearances, but none alas on *Chapter and Verse or Worse*.

162

Michael continued with his reviewing career for a few more years. He also developed a hankering for being involved in local politics and stood for town council in seven elections (polling respectively: 23, 112, 48, 101, 129, 56 and 68 votes. He then quite wisely listened to the electorate and stood no more.

Katy and Annabelle's busy schedules meant fewer and fewer family get-togethers, but they came as often as they could. They could both be found sometimes standing in the garden exchanging knowing glances, smiling to themselves. Katy's childhood tumble into the stream, real or manufactured, was long forgotten. Their own children were inducted into the secrets of the garden and decided to find it charming, if a little weird. The Captain and his band of men (and woman) (and possibly Eddie Fox) were less frequently seen as the years went by. Some dark nights in the dead of winter when all around was quiet they could still be heard by those with an attuned ear.

So, Michael and Judy lived on into ripening old age, content, satisfied and when time no longer had any meaning or use for them, they slipped quietly away from the world. They had left instructions for a humanist funeral for them both. Permission was sought and obtained for a garden burial and there they were laid to rest a few weeks apart. It is not known what Captain Edward De Vere Fox, Irish Meg, Silas and young Thomas et al (and possibly Eddie Fox) thought about this for they had not been consulted. Indeed, by this late stage they were even less rarely seen or heard. Such is life…well…you know what I mean.

The old house eventually became Jason's new house and when his children announced one summer evening that they had seen Great-Granddad and Great-Grandma in the garden he was not in the least surprised. Their imprint and spirit filled the house. Everyone said so.

But all that lay in the future.

"The best thing *we* ever did," said Judy one evening, as they sipped the obligatory (still) wine in the garden, "was to move to Lyme Regis."

Michael smiled.

"The best thing *I* ever did of course," added Judy, "was to meet and marry you.

"I was going to say exactly that."

"What? That the best thing I ever did was to meet and marry you?"

"Yes, you know how I always agree with you, especially when you are right."

"That day at Clapham Junction station. I often think about it. What if I hadn't had three cups of coffee? What if you weren't running late? But then you were always running late weren't you. You are my tardy hero and I adore you."

He kissed her. After all these years, it was still the appropriate response. It had never been anything, but the appropriate response to tell the truth.

He was happy. Judy was happy. Katy and Annabelle were happy. Everyone said so or at least everyone who cared said so.

In fact, not to put too fine a point on it, he was deliriously happy. It was not the first time he had felt deliriously happy, but it was the first time he really, really knew what it meant.

Even with his dodgy knees.

OPHELIA GET YOUR GUN

(AKA THERE IS SOMETHING ROTTEN IN THE STATE OF ARIZONA.)

ACT ONE SCENE ONE OUTSIDE THE SALOON BAR. A STAGECOACH IS SETTING DOWN ITS PASSENGERS.

OPHELIA (A GUNSLINGER): Well looky here, I espy a corncracker. Thou shouldst have stayed on yonder farm.

BILL HAMLET: Do you address me fair maiden? Your wit's too hot, it speeds too fast, 'twill tire. (IN AN ASIDE TO FELLOW PASSENGERS): She speaks, yet says nothing. (ADDRESSING OPHELIA): I am no farmer of this I can testify, you are guilty in your haste and ready wit to haze a tenderfoot.

ROSE ENCRANTZ (THE MAYORESS): Ophelia, durst you profess not to know this man. This is the fabled Bill Hamlet, this bold bad man turned good man. Like him that travels, he has returned again. The city's fathers have offered up the post of Sheriff to our friend here.

OPHELIA: He has a villainous low brow. He can be no friend of mine. There is a path of certain enmity between us.

BH: I grieve to hear you say it sweet Ophelia for I look upon your beauty as though I am in the first flush of youth, yes sirree.

OPHELIA: The man is false, he is a lowdown sneaking polecat who is intent on jawin' me to death. Mark my words people the next

166

thing you know he will be comparing me to a summer's day the lickspittle.

BH (IN AN ASIDE): She is a woman, therefore may be woo'd. She is a woman, therefore may be won. (ADDRESSING OPHELIA): That man that hath a tongue, I say, is no man, if with his tongue he cannot win a woman. You are a pretty red heifer and mean as catmeat but I wager I will tame you before the end of summer.

OPHELIA: Methink'st thou art a general offence and every man should beat thee. Thou appeareth nothing to me but a foul and pestilent congregation of vapours. You should be run out of town like the varmint you are.

BH: Yet, spaniel-like, the more she spurns my love, The more it grows and fawneth on her still. I love you with so much of my heart that none is left to protest. I pledge to thee that before the saguaro has withered and died we will have a hog-killin' time.

OPHELIA TAKES HER SIX-SHOOTER FROM HER HOLSTER AND FIRES A SHOT AT BILL HAMLET'S FEET. SHE WALKS OFF TO ADORING LOOKS FROM THE NEW SHERIFF.

OPHELIA GET YOUR GUN

(AKA THERE IS SOMETHING ROTTEN IN THE STATE OF ARIZONA.)

ACT THREE. SCENE FOUR. THE SALOON BAR IN TOMBSTONE

SHERIFF BILL HAMLET ENTERS STAGE LEFT

BH: Alack, I am distll'd almost to jelly with the act of fear. The James gang are without.

ROSE ENCRANTZ : Without what?

BH: The villains are once more abroad. O foul knaves. They seek their bloody revenge upon us.

RE: How so, sweet Sheriff? If they are abroad, how can they thus seek to harm us? Have thou been drinking moonshine again, brave protector of our town?

BH: They are here, their very flesh pollutes the OK Corral. And yet you speak as though you are unsifted in such perilous circumstances. Old man James of evil memory smiles and smiles, the smiling damned villain. That one may smile and smile and still be a villain, what calumny, what falseness and yet I fear it is so in Tombstone. Sweet Ophelia, wouldst thou save us from the very crack of doom which has opened up this very day, this cursed day?

OPHELIA: This cursed day, my lord Sheriff? The James gang are even now bedecked in chains of untold strength in the deepest foulest dungeons of the State penitentiary. Methinks your imaginations are as foul as Vulcan's stithy.

168

BH: Perhaps I am mad north-northwest, but I have seen what I have seen. Who will grant us deliverance from these men who wouldst treat us most cruelly? Sweet Ophelia, I beseech you once more.

OPHELIA: You, who have played me false these ten years past yet now thou durst seek my benevolence in taking arms against your sea of troubles? My brave Sheriff you must perforce look into your own soul for the deliverance you seek. I will have no part in't.

BH: Methinks the lady doth protest too much. I have a purse here which may yet turn your advantage to our own. Our own fair Rose, Mayoress of our beloved city has given me leave to rouse your spirits with the princely sum of twenty dollars.

RE: I have?

BH: Indeed, sweet lady. What sayest thou, Ophelia?

OPHELIA: Yeomen, bring me my Winchester73 that it may do honourable and bloody business this day.

THEY ALL EXIT STAGE LEFT. THERE ARE SOUNDS OF GUN PLAY AND A CRY OF: 'A HIT, A PALPBALE HIT'.

BOOT HILL CEMETERY LATER THAT DAY

BH: Lay her i' the earth and from her fair and unpolluted flesh may saguaro spring. Yes sirree.

THE REST IS SILENCE.

Acknowledgements and notes.

After completing 'A Twist of Lyme' in which we first encounter the Hamiltons I had no inkling at all that I would want to come up with another instalment. When I received my copies of the book, I knew I had to re-visit them. I had so much fun writing the first book and the second has been no exception. I just hope that you have found them has much fun to read. However, there will be no third instalment so we'll leave them to their lunch at the 'Prawn Cracker'. Rest assured they had a fabulous time.

You will search in vain for The Pint and Parrot on Ember Lane. It does not exist. There has been no reported landing of a UFO in Chipping Norton. Yet. Stammersson Inc does not exist in either Norway or England. The television shows within these pages may sound as though they should have been commissioned, but they haven't. Yet.

Please note that I cannot be held responsible if your Lemon Drizzle cakes or Gateaux Basque fail to live up to Elspeth's creations. But have a go anyway. And feel free to send samples.

If there is a veiled suggestion of Earlsfield being a hot-bed of crime…ignore it…it's not so. I am confident no one has ever been kidnapped and held hostage on Waynflete Street. I am equally confident that the flyover on Staines bypass (if indeed there is a flyover) holds no nasty surprises in its supporting pillars.

Once again, my thanks go to Gill who has re-visited the Hamiltons with me and once again, made valuable suggestions along the way, most of which I was only to willing to act on. However, any errors of any kind at all are down to me and I take full responsibility as much as I would like to blame someone else.

Thanks once more to Steve@MX Publishing and Bob@ Staunch for the customary and splendid help.

The appropriate response of course, is to kiss one of the above three folk. I'll let you decide just who that would be.

David Ruffle March 2014 Lyme Regis

Also from David Ruffle

Sherlock Holmes and The Lyme Regis Horror, and the sequels
Sherlock Holmes and The Lyme Regis Legacy and Sherlock
Holmes and The Lyme Regis Trials

Sherlock Holmes – Tales from the Stranger's Room
(Vol 1 and 2)
An eclectic collection of writings from twenty Holmes writers.

Also from David Ruffle

Sherlock Holmes and The Missing Snowman

A young girl's snowman has gone missing. Where can it have gone? There is only one man who can help. Sherlock Holmes, the most famous detective in the world.

www.mxpublishing.com